The Great Underground Empire

Story By

Thomas Knapp

I0626824

Based on MegaTokyo: Endgames By

Fred Gallagher

Editor

Ray Kremer

This one is for my friend, Nixia, who helps remind me from time to time that what I do here is a great privilege, and that I shouldn't waste all my time hating that I get the chance to do it.

(Oh, and do check out
The Regular Life of a Heavenly Beast,
so that she can learn that lesson as well.)

Chapter One: Dead History

The natural light generated by the mithril silver of the door dwindled rapidly, prompting Pirogoeth to invoke her light orb again, then positioning it three feet above her head for the most effective illumination. Not that there was particularly much to see at this point; merely battered, aged, faded brown bricks forming the floor, walls, and curved ceiling of the tunnel as it spiraled downward deeper into the earth.

What *was* remarkable was how well the descending hallway had stood the test of time. While there was little knowing exactly how long this particular hall had gone unattended, it must have been centuries at the very least judging from the thick dust being kicked up merely by the party's movements. Yet there was little sign that the ceiling or walls were in even in near imminent danger of collapse. There wasn't any bowing or significant cracks. No leaking mortar or obviously loose bricks.

Other ancient empires had not fared nearly as well, by Pirogoeth's understanding and experience. Kartage, for example, had been built on top of a major city of one such early empire, and what remained of that barely qualified as ruins. Had this not been a desperate attempt to end a major war, Pirogoeth would have been awestruck at the opportunity to engage in an unprecedented historical study.

That wistful feeling for what couldn't be only tugged stronger as the narrow hall emptied into a larger shaped cavern. Broad lines of mithril silver ran along the roof at least two hundred feet overhead, casting a dim white light to what had been a city within the Great Underground Empire.

It wasn't terribly large, which shouldn't have been surprising, no doubt the elven equivalent of a border town. But what really caught Pirogoeth's eye was the architecture of a city that no human had ever seen and lived to tell the tale. As the team slowly approached the city limits, awestruck by what they were looking at, Pirogoeth's eyes drank in the details of the nearest building.

It looked nothing like any human construction, circular buildings made of rings of carefully carved gray stone, still remarkably round and uncracked, stacked together tightly without any signs of mortar or cement, even with gaps cut into several rings to form windows with shimmering rainbow glass still perfectly intact.

The rings narrowed steadily as they stacked upward, with prongs like branches splitting out in several directions where they were topped with broad, domed, scaled emerald shingles. The craftsmen of Quan'Dor made trees out of stone to live in. It was both remarkable and yet unnerving, a sign of such a stagnant culture that they went to what must have been tremendous effort to replicate their old way of life rather than adapt to a new one.

Goat had a bit less reverence for the architecture than Pirogoeth did, running his hand along one ring and whistling. "Man, how do you suppose they did this, huh?"

"Shapers," Pirogoeth answered while Alyth nudged the scout back onto the center street. "It is believed that the ancient peoples used magic in far different ways than humans do now. Unlike the conjuring that is common today, the elves are believed to use their magic to shape what already existed."

"Sounds like a better form of magic to me," Wiglaf snorted.

Pirogoeth sniped back, "Perhaps if you have an irrational hatred of anything that isn't 'natural,' then yes it's better. If you're trying to survive in a war with fire mages burning down your forests... not so much."

Goat cut in, chirping happily, "Hey! Know what'd be fun? Having *this* argument again!"

Pirogoeth and Wiglaf glared at him, then at each other, before conceding the scout's point with silence.

The mage reluctantly acknowledged Goat was correct. There was little headway that could be made on that score at this point. Both her and Wiglaf were rather firmly entrenched in their opinion, and there was hardly anything that either could say to convince the other.

It's not that Pirogoeth could particularly *blame* Wiglaf for his scorn and distrust. It was far too easy for Pirogoeth to dismiss the fear of magic as the ignorant judgment of uneducated louts, like those common in the Central Free Provinces. They had little reason out of superstition to judge anyone with magical talents.

But for Wiglaf, nigh his entire people had been enslaved by the Winter Walker's domination magic; magic that he had personally witnessed Pirogoeth use herself. She could vow to never use it against him or any of the team, but what reason should he have to believe it? The fact that he's been willing to cooperate with her at all should be lauded.

"I..." she began.

Wiglaf turned his head in a huff. "How many times must I tell

6

you apologies are for the weak?"

"Fine then!" Pirogoeth replied indignantly. Two could play that passive-aggressive game.

She jogged to catch up with Jacques, who had the look of a man on high-alert. He asked, "Just how much *do* you know about this place, by the by?"

"About the empire specifically?" Pirogoeth quantified, "Next to nothing. I couldn't tell you where to go, if that's what you're asking. I know as much as can be known of the people of Quan'Dor and their history before going underground, but that's not going to be of much help, I'm sure."

"Taylor, I trust you're mapping our progress?" He asked the corpsman.

Taylor nodded, holding up his pad and pen. "Of course, sir."

"At least someone is useful," Jacques grumbled.

"Hey!" Goat protested, "When I hear something, I'll tell you! I'm just... not hearing anything but us."

"That *also* troubles me. I thought this entire underground was wrought with danger. I don't even see anything else *alive* down here."

Goat examined the light layer of dust and loose dirt upon the otherwise still pristine roadway, noting the long swaths and prints and marks upon the surface and said, "Well, there's definitely *something* down here. It's not like there's a wind to blow this stuff around. Whatever it is just isn't here *now*."

"Then how about we find somewhere else to be before whatever it is comes back?" Jacques suggested, using the silent consent of the rest of the team to push on towards the city center.

One thing Pirogoeth noticed about the city layout was that while the buildings were all unique in how they were constructed, much like the trees they were inspired by, the roads leading to the center were impeccably straight, and she suspected the curved roads that ran around the perimeter would be nigh perfect circles. She can't imagine *that* matched any pattern they would have been able to make in their above ground heavily forested homes.

It at least cast some doubt on the stagnant culture theory.

"As beautiful as everything still is, it's kinda hard to believe its a ghost town," Alyth said, her head as if on a swivel as her eyes drank in everything around her. "But it quite clearly is, isn't it? Not a soul to see or hear."

"Do we have any idea what happened to the people of Quan'Dor?" Taylor asked Pirogoeth.

The mage shook her head. "As I had said, Quan'Dor completely sealed themselves off from the rest of the world. At this point, elves are closer to myth than legend for most people of the continent. There's not even a consensus about what elves *looked like*, much less what happened to them in the depths of the earth."

She shrugged in defeat, and said, "Black hells, for all we know there are still elves running about down here, just not in this city. Not likely, of course, but not something that we can dismiss with what we know."

Aurora however, shook her head. "No. The elven people *are* gone. The only magic I feel is from artificial sources, like the lights above. My mother knew as well, somehow. She would always scoff at people who claimed to have seen an elf, and she would say that was because there were none left."

The healer sounded so very sad by that declaration, and Pirogoeth hugged her as she continued. "I... didn't want to believe her. I wanted to believe that the magic people still pranced about in the moonlight when people weren't watching, or played pranks on us in the fields, or... something other than... this."

"How did you mother know?" Pirogoeth wondered.

Aurora shook her head, "There's a lot of things my mother knew that I didn't. I wish she was still here."

The mage deciding learning more about Aurora's mother, a woman who supposedly possessed a black tome, was more intriguing than starting at stone trees. "I know you don't like to talk about it... but what happened to her? How did she pass on?"

The healer had *always* clammed up when this question came around before, but Pirogoeth was hoping more familiarity with her would loosen her tongue. Which it did, somewhat, though not in the way that the mage was expecting.

"I'm... afraid you'll think I'm crazy," Aurora admitted, her voice timid.

Alyth imposed herself into the conversation reassuringly. "Honey, we travel with Mikael here. Coders, if sanity was a requirement for this team, half of us wouldn't make the cut and the other half would be committed before they even got the chance to enlist."

"We *are* traveling through unknown territory filled with any number of potential horrors, all to do battle with mages beyond the peer of any mortal currently alive," Jacques added. "Just how sane do you think we are?"

8

Aurora responded with a tired giggle, and finally relented. "It quite literally just... happened. I was healing an injured deer on the foothills just south of the mountains, about a week east of the Snake River. There wasn't a town within days travel at least. It was almost two years ago at this point. She called my name... but I didn't respond right away. I... I... figured healing the deer could come first."

She sniffled as she continued, "Because of that, I... almost missed her leaving. She was already in fade by the time I got there. I cried so much... begged her not to go... but she told me she was being called, and she couldn't disobey. I... barely had any time to say goodbye before she faded entirely."

"Faded? Could you explain?" Pirogoeth asked.

Aurora shrugged as she wiped her eyes, "I'm not sure how else to say it. She faded away into nothing. She was being called. It was her time to go. In her last moments, she told me to take her tome and hide it away. That I could come back and get it if the guiding spirits deemed I was ready."

"Your mother was Chosen?" Pirogoeth asked.

Aurora nodded, then winced as she admitted, "So... so am I. I sometimes, rarely, hear the voice of the spirit in my head, influencing me in certain directions. It was the one that told me to accept conscription, as much as I didn't want to."

The healer panicked and hastily whimpered, "Please don't think I'm insane! It's true! I'm not crazy!"

Pirogoeth jumped to comfort her, hugging Aurora around the waist and saying gently, "*I* don't think you're crazy at all. I... have the same thing. I'm Chosen as well... at least that's what my master and his peers call this phenomenon. There *are* spirits that reside beyond this world, and they sometimes lead us down paths we wouldn't normally take. I'm here for much the same reason as you are."

Aurora's hopeful tone matched the glistening in her eyes, "You... do? You are?"

Pirogoeth nodded in confirmation. "It's rarely anything strong, like a coherent voice in my head, though it certainly *can* be. If you're crazy, then so am I."

Wiglaf grunted, and Pirogoeth's eyebrows furrowed in annoyance expecting a barb from the Dayne shaman. He even acknowledged that as he said, "As much as I would love to follow that judgment to its conclusion, I instead have to admit that you two mages aren't the only ones to have such influence. Or do you think that I would decide to travel south and try to appeal to your kind completely

9

of my own volition?"

Taylor exhaled heavily, "While I can't say I've ever felt guided down a certain path, it would certainly explain my seemingly random wanderlust. The Church of the Coders liked to talk about predestination, and I just chalked it up to that, but this explanation... feels right."

Alyth and Goat looked at each other guiltily, then Goat quipped, "I knew there was something between us all this time!"

The marksman stomped down on the scout's right foot so hard he winced, and she said, "Mikael and I... have had this discussion before. More than once. Serendipity he called it. Can't say I've ever heard voices, but I can certainly agree with the feeling that something pushed me into certain choices in my life."

Tyronica bit her lip, "I always wondered how I had an uncanny sense to find trouble to fight after leaving Aramathea. I had heard Dominus Socrato talk about 'Chosen' people before... but I had never really considered *I* was one."

Jacques scoffed, "I kinda figured *all* of us were. The Gold Pirates were *filled* with Chosen people. That influence is one that tends to spur people towards adventure."

"Does that mean you are too?" Goat asked.

The sergeant huffed. "If I am, I've followed what was expected of me so well that it's never been an issue. Probably am, though. I'm not losing any sleep over it regardless. What I *am* losing sleep over is where exactly we're going to go from here. Because something tells me the roads through this empire don't exactly take straight lines through the underground."

The party had reached the center circle of the city, and a stone marker with four green signs emblazoned with ruby lettering. Two pointed north-northeast, another due north, and the fourth east. All four bore characters that were presumably the ancient language of the Quan'Doran people.

While Jacques's question was ostensibly for the group, his eyes were focused on Pirogoeth. "Anyone, by chance, able to read ancient languages?"

"Not *this* old." Pirogoeth replied. "What few pieces I might remember wouldn't be of much use."

Aurora, however, was able to supply something resembling an answer. She pointed along the north path and said, "I think that way would be a good start."

Jacques invited her to continue. "And why is that?"

"I can feel the flow of magic strongest in that direction. It heads to the source of the magical flow. The other paths weaken. This one get stronger."

Pirogoeth nodded, "It would *have* to be a hub of some sort, or at least *lead* to that hub." Then with a bolt of inspiration, the mage added, "And once there, *I* could do the rest!"

"And how is that?" Jacques asked.

"This entire empire is effectively powered by an artificial ley line network," Pirogoeth explained. "This is the flow of power I tapped into when I scryed the Winter Walkers. At the center, where the power can be more readily tapped, I could do it again and memorize the layout of the network, then match it up with our maps of the surface. If Wiglaf is right, one of those paths in the network should lead somewhere around... Vazmeade, was it?"

Wiglaf nodded, but didn't say anything, instead settling on suspicious, narrowed eyes in the mage's direction.

Jacques didn't give anyone the opportunity to voice objections to that plan. "Then we have a course of action. Follow me, folks. If you want to scout ahead Goat, you can... but something tells me we'll see anything coming quite easily."

That was true enough. There weren't trees or rolling hills or other obstructions within the caverns of the underground empire. The cavern they were in was broad and flat, and while there were rough cave structures pockmarked into the cavern walls, those were so far away that anything that emerged from them would be spotted with an hour of warning at least.

The trek to the pass Aurora had pointed out made Pirogoeth appreciate the sheer scale of this cavern, and presumably the rest within the Great Underground Empire. It took hours just to reach the mouth of the tunnel; if tunnel was really the proper word for it. The ceiling barely dropped as the walls narrowed, but even then the walls would have had enough room for at least five merchant carts to move side by side.

"Someone didn't want congestion on their roads," Alyth quipped.

"Clearly," Pirogoeth replied absentmindedly, her mind already mulling over possibilities for what she was seeing. As far as she could tell, the infrastructure of Quan'Dor was largely intact... though by the evidence, no one had lived in this city for some time.

The emptiness and painful uniformity of their surroundings had allowed Pirogoeth's mind to wander. Where did the elves go? Had they simply died out? That seemed unlikely. She figured they would have stumbled across some remains. Had they simply moved to other places in the empire? That was also hard to believe... they'd have revisited this part of their empire at some point relatively recently, if for no reason than to explore it.

It was a mystery, and one potentially vital to their success in navigating the underground. If the stories Goat told about previous explorers was true, whatever had purged the elves from this place still lingered, and if they couldn't solve this mystery, chances are it would claim her and her team as well.

"Whoa! Look at that!"

Goat's exclamation startled the mage, and she was already reaching into her tome before she processed what he had seen.

A mere sparklebunny, its pelt shimmering in the silvery light above and creating a muted rainbow aura around it as it hopped frantically towards the burrow that it had made for itself.

Pirogoeth pulled her hand away from her tomes and snarled, "Really? *That* got you worked up?"

Goat grinned nervously, "Just... didn't expect to see something like that down here."

The mage rolled her eyes and steadied her breath. "Of course you didn't, though you shouldn't be surprised. Chimeric magic, fusing two beings together, was *also* an area of expertise of the people of Quan'Dor. While us humans have been able to draw curses that do something similar, the people of Quan'Dor could do things with merging that we can't even *begin* to figure out how they did it."

They could manipulate things that shouldn't be... like the minute crystals in the fur of sparklebunnies that give them their distinctive prismatic coloring... or the pockets of air in bubble buffaloes that make them so much lighter and nimble than their normal cousins... or rockbears... or any combination you can dream of. Any chimeric beast you have encountered in your lives outside of the natural chimeras caused by metaphysical creatures can draw near a direct line to the shaping of the elven peoples."

She looked back at the sparklebunny burrow as the group continued on, "And we just might see any of those creatures, and even many we've never seen before, down here."

As she finished her mini-lecture, her mind began drifting back to the apparent disappearance of the elves, and the idea of chimeric creatures no human had ever set eyes on. History suggested that as the ancient war became more desperate for the elven peoples, their chimeras became increasingly more aggressive and dangerous. Rockbears, for example, came much later than sparklebunnies.

Could the people of Quan'Dor, after their retreat underground, created something out of their own fear, desperation, and hubris that they could not control?

And if so... what could it have been?

"What is on your mind, Pirogoeth?" Tyronica asked, seeing the mage's deep thought.

"Nothing of substance, I'm afraid. Merely running through possibilities and contemplation with very little conclusive evidence that could possibly prepare us for anything."

"There's no number of monsters that could be down here, from even before the elves moved underground." Aurora confirmed. "If the stories my mother told were true, at least. I shudder to think that any of them are accurate."

And yet *another* possibility Pirogoeth hadn't considered. There were no end of nightmarish creatures that had existed in the depths at one time, and possibly still did. Trolls, stoneater worms, flame and lava demons... it was even thought that some dragons may have formed lairs in the deeps away from the increasing presence of mortals. Could Quan'Dor have dug too deep and found something lost to everything but nightmares?

"How about we save the ghost stories for tonight when we've set up camp?" Jacques suggested.

Tyronica snorted, then looked up to the shining lines of mithril silver above. "Presuming there even *is* such a thing as tonight in this hole."

It turned out that there was, as several hours later as they emerged into the next cavern, the lights from above slowly started to dim, starting from the east and slowly creeping westward.

"Fascinating," Taylor said as he watched the phenomenon. "They managed to simulate a self-perpetuating day and night cycle."

Jacques assessed their situation, seeing that the next city was several hours away, and then noting the presence of a handful of smaller elven houses much closer and detached from the larger town. He pointed in the direction of the nearest three and asked, "Well, folks, do you want to pitch some tents on this rocky ground, or do you wanna see if we can't find something more comfortable in there?"

Pirogoeth didn't expect much debate on the topic. Even Wiglaf didn't issue a protest, claiming that only a fool sleeps on stone when a better option could be found. Even more remarkable was that she managed to hold her tongue about his deviation from a "natural" life style. Let no one say that she couldn't be prudent.

The mage expected that elven houses wouldn't have doors or locks in the way that humans come to understand them. The doors themselves were almost indistinguishable from the rest of the buildings, the only indicator that they were different from the rest of the exterior being that the cut in the stacked rings wasn't present. There was no handle or doorknob, nor any sign of hinges or guides to indicate how the door even opened.

She also expected that Aurora might be able to trigger whatever magical lock had been placed on the doors, which had been correct. The healer had nervously approached, sensing the energies that had been used to secure the home, then held out her hand and touched the center, where the hand print momentarily glowed before the door slid backward then to the right.

What Pirogoeth *hadn't* expected was being able to the same. On a lark, the mage attempted to do the same thing, even though she couldn't sense the elven magic herself. To her surprise, the attempt worked, the hand print glowed, and the door slid open without the slightest fuss about who had done the opening.

She pointed at the third house, and said, "Goat. Try opening that one."

The scout complied, though unlike Pirogoeth and Aurora, his attempt met with no success.

Jacques slinked up behind her, and said, "What are you two doing?"

"Research," Pirogoeth replied. "It doesn't particularly matter, as there should be plenty enough space in both houses, but I was curious. It's fascinating how the magic locks merely aren't just personalized, but also it doesn't seem to matter what type of magical talent you have at all. Just any type of magic will do, it seems."

"Is that right?" Jacques said, his eyes taking on that glazed over expression of a man that really didn't care, but knew that further extrapolation was coming whether he liked it or not.

"It's a fascinating look into an ancient culture, one that we know distressingly little about. A simple magic seal, with no specific restrictions. Enough to keep potentially dangerous animals out, but allow any elven person in. It's quite possible that the people of Quan'Dor didn't have the same concepts of personal property or space that us humans do."

And the matter that I could open these doors, even though

there would be no reason for me to do so. The magic of elves and humans was markedly different, and it seems unusual that they wouldn't distinguish between the two as they created their homes. Could their magics have deteriorated over time? Or would such specifics require more effort than they were willing to invest, figuring that if human mages that could open these doors had invaded their lands that the empire was so broken as to make no difference?"

Jacques gently nudged her inside, then motioned for Goat and Tyronica to follow. "You *do* remember this is a wartime operation and not an archaeological study, right?"

"There's nothing wrong with making note of the things we find while on the way," Pirogoeth replied. "And learning some of those hints could potentially be useful the deeper into the empire we go."

"Really?"

"The people of Quan'Dor went *somewhere*," she insisted, "And they didn't die here."

There was considerable evidence of that, or more accurately lack thereof. Had the elves faced extinction, it hadn't happened in this house at least. There were no bodies. There were no signs of struggle that would suggest fighting. There was no chaos that would suggest ransacking from an increasingly desperate people. Just thin layers of dust around a reasonably neat homestead.

Elven furniture was certainly different than anything she had seen before. She ran a finger along the narrow armrest of what appeared to be a sofa or futon, trying to brush away the dust to reveal its true color. Brilliant silver, even after all this time, forming an elaborate curved frame in which the back and seat were all one piece.

The frame itself looked almost like the skeleton of the thick, solid wooden furniture she was familiar with, with about half of the padding she had seen even in regards to Aramathean style. On top of that, she figured there was maybe three inches of clearance between the floor and the seat of the sofa. How could that have possibly been comfortable?

The upper "branches" of the home revealed more of the same, three bedrooms with hammocks that while not impeccably made weren't exactly disheveled like people in a rush.

Tyronica scoffed at the furnishings, and said, "I don't think I'd be able to sleep on that."

Pirogoeth agreed with that assessment. The mage would probably fit in one of the hammocks, but she'd be the only one.

"Looks like Pirogoeth gets some manner of comfort then,"

Jacques said, "Lucky her. Goat, think this is a good scouting point?"

Goat spun around, "Yeah... between the windows I think I could get a good eye and ear on the surroundings."

"Good. I'm gonna hop across to the others and make sure they're set up well. We'll move... when the lights turn up again, I guess?"

The lights above hadn't completely died, still providing a faint glow similar to moonlight, and Pirogoeth figured if the elves had mimicked a day-night cycle, they probably mimicked a seasonal cycle as well. "That could be almost half the day spent here, you know?"

The sergeant huffed, "Probably. But I don't want us stumbling about in low-light conditions until we have a better feel for the lay of the land."

That was hardly unfair, considering Pirogoeth needed to conjure her light orb just to clearly see Jacques's face at that point.

Once Jacques left, Goat asked, "Could you... put that out, please? I would like to adapt my eyes to the dark, and I can't do that with your light glowing like that."

"Oh! Sorry!" Pirogoeth yelped, dismissing the cantrip and letting darkness reclaim the interior of the elven home.

She more heard the smile in Goat's voice than saw it when said, "So, *now* we can tell ghost stories?"

Tyronica tried to hold back her chuckle so as not to encourage the scout, and mostly failed. "I fear that any tales we could tell might not even hold water to the reality. For all we know there are trolls down here that have been wandering the underground and devouring anyone who dares enter."

"Trolls? Haven't they been extinct for centuries?" Goat asked.

Pirogoeth shrugged, "They were found mere ten years ago on the Gibraltar Islands during the big mining rush, and in underground caves and caverns much like these. It's *possible*, I suppose."

There was good reason to be scared of those monsters. The advice for even the most seasoned combat veterans was that fighting a troll was something that should only be done in the most desperate of situations. The strength and size of five men, the agility of a cat, hide thicker than most heavy armor, and if all that wasn't enough, an inhuman regenerative ability that closed nearly any wound in a matter of seconds. Only a fire or acid bath could reliably finish a troll, neither of which were usually found in abundance on most adventurers.

Pirogoeth then expressed her reservations about that idea. "But... trolls aren't neat, and it's not like they're ambush hunters. If this

16

was a troll's doing, the door would be embedded halfway into the opposite wall, and the entire interior would look like it had been painted by Palloch during his crimson phase."

Goat blinked, not getting the reference. Tyronica gagged, as she did. "Dominus Socrato still has those splatterings, I take it?" the Aramathean woman asked after her throat stopped convulsing.

"Yep," Pirogoeth replied. "And they're just as ugly as you remember, I'm sure."

"Okay, so if no trolls, then what?" Goat asked.

The mage shook her head, "There's no way of knowing with the lack of evidence, and as I said earlier, I'm not going to work any of you up with wild theories. It could literally be *anything* at this point from elementals to elves waiting in the very next town over."

Jacques returned and interjected into the conversation, "And that'll be an anything we can talk about in the morning. Goat, you get the first watch. Then Tyronica, then me. If it's still too dark, Goat'll take over again."

"What about me?" Pirogoeth asked. Jacques had never exempted her from watch duty before.

"I want you as alert as possible as we are actually out and about. Which means you get the blessing of avoiding late night watches for the near future. Enjoy your sleep, because I suspect you're gonna need it."

"Pick a hammock! Not like any of us are gonna be using them!" Goat suggested with a smile.

Pirogoeth figured she might as well try it. Normally the idea of sleeping in something that had to have been hundreds of years old at least would be something she'd dismiss immediately. But everything else she had seen in the Great Underground Empire had seemed to stand the test of time.

And it was worth the chance of avoiding having to sleep in that battered bedroll the militia had given her.

She chose the east most bedroom, as it was farthest away from Goat's position and allowing her to conjure a little bit of light to work her way around.

It was amazing how empty the room was, just the hammock mounted to three corners of the room approximately a foot off the floor, and a cabinet seemingly made of shaped pearl in the fourth. The cabinet only went up to her waist, and couldn't have held more than maybe a couple changes of clothes... though if their garments were as durable as everything else, maybe a couple changes were all they needed.

She pulled open both shelves, not terribly surprised to find them mostly empty. Yet further evidence that whoever lived here wasn't taken by surprise. She tossed herself into the hammock with a disappointed sigh, waiting for the bouncing to settle before she dispelled her light and closed her eyes.

But with her mind filled almost to the brim contemplating the mystery in front of her, she doubted she was going to get much sleep.

~   ~   ~

And she didn't... just not for the reason she had been expecting.

Pirogoeth didn't even remember exactly when she fell asleep to begin with. Just that she was being gently shaken and Tyronica's hushed voice asking her to wake.

The outside was starting to brighten enough that the lights streaming in from the window near blinded her, and as she blinked rapidly to try and adjust, she asked groggily, "What... what's going on?"

"I apologize for waking you. Goat and Jacques want you to see something. I'm not sure what. I just got up myself, and I don't see anything out there."

With a resigned sigh, Pirogoeth slid out of the hammock and straightened her clothes before following Tyronica to the opposite room in the dwelling. The two men were waiting at the window, staring out intently, and Pirogoeth asked, "What in the Coders are you two looking at?"

Goat grabbed her by her left bicep, and swung her towards the window, his head hovering over hers. "Just wait for it... I bet it's going to happen pretty soon."

"What's going to happen?" She asked in annoyance.

"Goat saw something out there, and he got my attention where I saw it too. We were hoping you might have an idea what hell we're looking at." Jacques said. "Whatever it is started moving around as the lights started getting brighter, and now there's at least five of them wandering about out there."

Pirogoeth was of Tyronica's mind. She couldn't see anything. "You think I'll be able to identify it?"

Jacques shrugged. "Maybe."

Goat's hand thrust out over Pirogoeth's head and to the left. "Over there!" he hissed, "Look!"

Pirogoeth followed the scout's extended finger, and followed the direction to the glimmer of a sparklebunny's pelt occasionally catching the simulated daylight as it hopped towards one of the many caves that dotted "You mean... behind the rabbit?" she asked sarcastically.

"Yes!" Goat replied. "Here it comes!"

And this time, she saw it. One spindly, mottled gray leg shot out from around the perimeter of the dwelling, and neatly skewered the sparklebunny through the back before dragging it back into the cave.

Stepping out into the light, it came into view one leg at a time, eight in all and bearing the body of an extremely large spider, at least ten feet from the abdomen to the head.

But it was the head that caught Pirogoeth's attention. Instead of the usual thorax of a spider was the front half of a bull instead, with a head that seemed to blend the two distinct animals. A row of eight eyes circled the front of the bull face, crowned by a pair of long, curved, near pitch black sharpened horns that protruded from the temple, and four equally black fangs that stuck out from the lower lip and below the creature's jaw line where half of the prey animal now hung lifelessly from.

The rear half, or at least one of the back legs, was sticking out of the maw of a smaller companion creature, possibly a juvenile considering the less developed fangs and horns along with a significantly smaller size. Still more emerged from other caves at roughly the same time, seeming to forage around for food. There weren't many, at most twenty... but that was about twenty too many for Pirogoeth's tastes.

Pirogoeth's mind started whirling as she processed evidence that might explain one of the major mysteries of the Great Underground Empire. Could *that* have been the cause of the elven disappearance? Or at least a factor in it?

"What do you think?" Jacques asked.

Pirogoeth shook her head. "Whatever they are... they're not trolls."

Chapter Two: By The Light of the Moon

In light of the party's discovery, Jacques changed their plans, especially as they noticed that the creatures retreated entirely upon the shift to "night", with not even the slightest sign of venturing out of their cave dens once the lights started dimming.

Jacques wasn't swayed by any theories that whatever those creatures were, they largely stayed off the main roads, and didn't seem to be the slightest bit concerned about the party, even as several creatures came right up to the dwelling the team was camped in. Jacques wasn't going to tempt fate, especially as they found evidence of more of those creatures roaming the caverns.

"Aye... the spidulls been here too," Goat confirmed, matching the scrapes in the dust with what he figured were the shuffling gait that the creatures they were getting glimpses of must use to move around on such gangly legs.

They were in the center of yet another abandoned elven town, five days into their excursion. It suggested that the creatures weren't an isolated phenomenon, and more likely than not were present all throughout the underground. It also confirmed that the creatures were much bolder in their movements the deeper into the empire the party went.

"Bullders," Alyth countered. "Spidulls is just... dull."

The two had been going back and forth on what to call the chimeric monsters they had seen since yesterday, ever since Goat tried to coin the name "Spidull."

"And Bullders is a load of bull," Goat countered.

"Where to next, Aurora?" Jacques asked the healer, willfully ignoring the bickering. "Make it quick, because I do *not* want to be here once day breaks."

This time, however, the healer didn't have an answer. The road split from the center of town in three directions, all of them vaguely heading north. "They all... feel like they go towards the center. I think we're close."

It was Wiglaf who provided a suggestion. The Wolf Shaman had been spying Taylor's map making progress from over the corpsman's shoulder, and asked, "Is this accurate?"

"Well, not perfectly, I'm sure," Taylor answered, "I'm not exactly performing precise cartography here."

"But close enough," Wiglaf pressed, "In terms of distances

and direction."

"Yes... I've tried to do that, certainly, and I'm sure this is a reasonably good estimate..."

By that point, the Dayne was no longer paying attention, his eyes narrowed in though, muttering quietly to himself as his focus drifted to the northwest. "I think I know where we are," he said, raising his hand to point out the direction, "And if I'm right, we might want to go that way."

"Why do you say that?" Jacques queried.

Wiglaf, perhaps understandingly, was annoyed by the suspicion. "The other mage said that all of them go in the same direction, right? We're underneath Daynish lands now. I know directions here slightly better than any of you, I'm sure."

"Been underneath Daynish lands often?" The sergeant shot back, the tension in his voice rising.

Pirogoeth cut in, trying to defuse the situation. "Aurora already said she doesn't have a preference, sir. And I'm sure Wiglaf *does* have a better awareness of what is likely overhead. There's no harm in following his suggestion."

"Pardon me if I want to know how he came to that decision."

"You've never asked Aurora or me to justify ourselves," the mage noted.

Wiglaf growled, "I don't need you defending me, *mage*. If I am correct, we are near to Mirror Lake. The elven people would have needed to get water somewhere, and I would bet Mirror Lake would be an easy place to tap into. It wouldn't hurt to top off our own supply."

"And *that* makes sense," Jacques agreed. "Let's move, people. I want to get water and get to cover before 'daybreak' if at all possible."

Pirogoeth rolled her eyes in annoyance. Why did she even bother trying to support this jerk?

"It is inevitable that we will have to fight these creatures we are avoiding eventually," Wiglaf said as they past the city limits, and Jacques started scanning the surroundings towards the walls at the caves dotting the cavern stone, and up towards the lights in anticipation of the shift to the underground's daytime.

"Perhaps," Jacques countered, "But for now, as long they're keeping to the day and giving us the night, I'm going to respect those boundaries. We have enough of a fight waiting for us if we ever get out of here. No sense picking more if we don't have to."

Wiglaf grunted in disapproval, but didn't push the issue farther, striding ahead to take the lead and increase their pace towards the connecting tunnel they had chosen to take. The Dayne didn't think the road was far, and the rest of the team hoped his instincts were correct... because the walls of *this* particular tunnel narrowed farther than any one previous.

"Ya know, after all the wide roads, this actually feels cramped, even though it's probably still bigger than your average trade lane," Alyth remarked. "I don't like this anyway."

"Just get right up close to me!" Goat offered, wincing as the marksman elbowed him in response.

"In your dreams, maybe."

Goat shook his head, "No, in my dreams you're..."

Alyth then shoved him roughly, causing him to stumble then fall onto his rump. "You're disgusting," she growled. "Can't you take this seriously?"

The scout hopped to his feet, and replied, "I'm regarding the situation with all the seriousness it deserves, I'll have you know!"

"Then why don't you show it?"

"I am!"

Jacques cut in, trying to keep the amusement out of his voice, with some success. "There's not a single burrow in this tunnel."

Goat added on, "And no other signs that anyone or thing has been this way in a while."

But then the sergeant chided, "But that *doesn't* mean we should let our guard completely down. Who knows what else poses a risk down here?"

Wiglaf then pulled up quickly, his right arm out to hold the team. "Wait... you smell that?"

Pirogoeth did, at least. Not that she expected anyone else would miss it. After almost a week getting used to the sterile, dusty, earthy smells of the underground, their noses quickly picked up on the scent of damp, fresh air from ahead. Could there be another unknown opening to the Great Underground Empire?

Their formation fell apart as the entire team broke into a sprint, any fatigue forgotten. Pirogoeth was simply impressed that she managed to keep up, merely falling back maybe five strides at best before they reached the opening to the surface world again.

At least... technically.

There had been no mithril silver gate blocking this particular egress, no doubt because it would have been completely unnecessary. The party had emerged out onto what was more like a boardwalk, granted made with brick rather than wood, carved into the rock to create an overhang that entirely blocked the view from anyone who might have been above.

Wiglaf approached a railing shaped from granite, still able to hold his weight as he leaned forward. "This is indeed Mirror Lake, though from a vantage I've never seen before."

Pirogoeth found it was easier to kneel down and look between the bars of the railing, her eyes widening as she processed what she was seeing. Through the surprisingly clear water that had pooled at the bottom a good hundred feet below, she caught the image of the waxing moon above, which reflected and cast a slightly distorted image onto the rock above. "The entire lake bed is effectively one massive plate of silver!"

"Well, I guess they don't call it Mirror Lake for nothing," Alyth remarked, following their lead as she got a look herself. "And you can stop pretending you're not looking at my butt, Mikael."

"I'm not," the scout retorted. Confirming his claim, he was actually looking up, leaning dangerously forward onto his toes to try and get a glimpse of anything above the outcropping. "You can't see the top from here at all. Think about that, for however knows how long, people could have been perched at the top of these cliffs, and never known the elven people were walking about underneath them."

"That's not surprising," Pirogoeth said, "This entire lake is believed to be the caldera of a massive volcano, perhaps from even before the time of the Coders forming the world as we know it. The top is several thousand feet above and made of very sharp, jagged, and treacherous volcanic rock. I doubt even the Daynes would have risked the attempt to climb down it particularly often."

"If my people had, I heard of no successful attempts," Wiglaf acknowledged, "It's likely also why the elves felt safe enough to create this unprotected trail into the surface world."

Aurora had moved further ahead with Tyronica, and the healer shouted, "Friends! Over here!"

The rest of the team rushed to the sound, stopping as the trail widened into what was the elven equivalent of a resort town. A massive stone tree dwelling forty feet thick marked the center of the cleared out space, as large as any dwelling they had seen up to that point, with what looked like at least a hundred branched rooms that spread across the center of the clearing.

Jacques clicked his tongue, and Pirogoeth could hear the relief in his voice. "Well... we have a place to camp out for the day... just in case we need the shelter." The former pirate had not been keen on sleeping out in the open, even if there was no sign that any creepy beast within the underground had come this way.

Tyronica had returned to the group, and beckoned them to follow her. "There's more than shelter here..." she said cryptically as she took the lead, back onto the road that followed the perimeter of the lake. After another hundred feet, the road opened up into another clearing dotted with a series of secluded grottoes, each with individual waterfalls heated no doubt from the heart of the volcano kicking up small clouds of steam that billowed up the top of the chamber.

"Warm baths as well," the Aramathean soldier said with a smile.

Alyth looked upon the sight and said wistfully, "I would kill every single damn one of you for one of those right now."

"I would kill every single one of them to *see* you in one of those right now," Goat quipped.

Alyth sighed in defeat, "I'm just too tired and want a bath too badly to hurt you."

Jacques coughed to get his team's attention. "Alright, how about we set up camp, and then if it looks like the coast is clear, we'll rotate in some bath time."

With that promise in mind, the party made their return to the massive tree dwelling. Unlike any other elven building they had seen, there was no "lock" on the main door, but there were on each individual "room," confirming the theory that this was some sort of community space, the elven equivalent of an inn or hotel. Pirogoeth and Aurora went about the matter of opening enough doors for everyone, where a potentially disastrous discovery was made.

There was a knock from the room that Pirogoeth had opened for Goat, followed by his slightly muffled voice saying, "Problem."

"What's that?" Jacques asked.

"I... can't get out."

From the other side of the trunk in another room, Tyronica agreed, "The door won't open from this side."

The sergeant looked questioningly at Aurora and Pirogoeth, both of whom shrugged defensively. "Apparently, the elves didn't discriminate just how their locks worked?" Pirogoeth offered uncertainly.

"We are regarding a people who were inherently magical by default," the healer added. "They might not have seen any *need* to be so specific with how their doorways sealed. Anyone inside would have had the same magical talent to get in, after all."

Pirogoeth offered as a theory, "Perhaps we never really noticed because Aurora and I have been close enough to the doors to 'unlock' the seal?"

"Or the locks in this dwelling work differently because it's more public by design?" Aurora countered.

Goat interrupted the thought experiment by saying, "While that's all well and good, there's barely enough room in here for me to lay down, much less anyone else. Except maybe Alyth if she was willing to sleep on top of me."

"Keep dreaming," the marksman growled.

"Aurora, let Goat and Tyronica out," Jacques ordered. "Pirogoeth, you come with me while we examine the higher levels. If this is anything like the hotels we know, there will be larger rooms and suites higher up."

She complied, falling in step with the sergeant as he started up the spiraling staircase. It would be another three floors before they found what they were looking for, a pair of larger multiple room suites that would suit the party's needs. "I don't like being this far off the ground," Jacques said with distaste. "Makes us too easily cornered... but being able to muster quickly is more important, so there's nothing for it."

He then leaned down over the stairwell, and shouted, "Alright! Get up here, folks!"

Pirogoeth couldn't recall the group being so quick to act since they entered the underground. She understood *why* of course, it was the same reason she staked a spot in one corner before the rest of the team had even reached the proper floor. She had no doubt she smelled as earthy as the empire itself, and the thought of getting cleaned up was nigh intoxicating.

And Jacques noticed it too. "Alright, you all win," he said, relenting to the desires of his team. "We'll go to the baths in groups. I'll keep watch until everyone is finished, then I'll have someone take over so I can clean up? Sound good?"

Pirogoeth immediately said, "I'll wait for everyone else to have theirs."

Truth was, she wasn't the least bit comfortable bathing around others, despite such public bathing houses being a social event that Aramathean citizens were known to occasionally enjoy. She had never warmed to the practice even after the few times she had participated before simply bowing out of public bathing entirely.

"Anyone else have privacy issues?" Jacques asked, "I'd rather not spend all night doing this."

Aurora got a dangerous twinkle to her eye, and flashed a teasing smile in Alyth's direction before looping her arm over Goat's elbow. "While they decide, would you like to join me, Goat? Then we can switch when I'm done?"

The scout smiled broadly, and replied, "Why I would *love* to. Far be it for a true gentleman to refuse such a kind request."

"The next time you're gentlemanly would be the first," Alyth snorted.

Aurora at this point couldn't be laying it on any thicker if you had given her cream, starch, and a spatula. With a hand over her mouth like she had been scandalized, she said, "Oh my... then you might need to watch us after all, sergeant. I'm not sure I'd be able to control myself with such a ruffian nearby. Bad boys have always been my weakness."

Whatever direction this game was going, Jacques wanted no part of it. "Leave me out of this."

"I'll keep watch," Wiglaf grunted, "If for no reason than to get this over with."

Aurora spun about, arm still linked around Goat's as they took the lead down the stairs, Wiglaf just behind. After several seconds, Alyth's jaw clenched, and she dashed to the stairwell.

"I know what you're doing!" She shouted in annoyance. "It's not going to work!"

The marksman then stomped off angrily to her chosen crash space, grumbling to herself. Jacques paid her no mind, addressing the rest of the team. "Tyronica, you, Taylor and Alyth will go once those three come back. I'll keep watch for you all then Pirogoeth can have her alone time."

The mage flushed in embarrassment, and that got the old pirate to smile, "Oh, don't be all sheepish. Some people don't like being vulnerable like that. Hell, one of the perks I loved about being first mate was my own washbasin so that I didn't have to share a bucket with the rest of the crew. You've earned the special treatment."

"I'll keep an eye out for you if you'd like, sir," Taylor offered.

Jacques gave him a wary eye, and say, "More like you're hoping to catch a view of our mage in the buff."

"Not like he'd have to be sneaky about *that*, sir," Alyth snarked from inside her assigned suite.

That earned a chuckle and a sly response of, "That's true enough."

This turn in the direction of the discussion wasn't helping the color in Pirogoeth's cheeks any, especially since Taylor wasn't showing any discomfort at all.

"I would never assume," the corpsman said. "Only on invitation."

The mage ducked her head, mumbled, "Okay, gonna go die now," and retreated to her crash space as fast as she could without running.

She jumped face down into the hammock, the swaying motion that created feeling like it was trying to rock her to sleep. It did seem to have some sort of calming effect, because she had forgotten that she had chosen to share the same suite with Alyth until the marksman spoke up.

"You *do* realize getting so worked up over something so obvious just encourages us to tease you *more*, right?"

The mage snapped her head up, regretting the motion when the back of her neck flared up angrily. Alyth looked more bemused than anything as she further said, "Honestly. No one blames you. Taylor's a fine looking man, and certainly has that sophisticated charm, doesn't he?"

"You're not helping," Pirogoeth retorted. "Besides, shouldn't you be worrying about what Aurora is doing with Goat right now?"

The marksman snorted, "Hardly. Aurora been trying to 'get me to admit my feelings' for the better part of the last four days. You haven't been bunked with us, so you haven't been hearing her go on about it."

It wasn't so much that Pirogoeth wanted to delve into Alyth's love life as much as she was looking for any opportunity to keep attention off of herself. "And what feelings are those?"

The marksman sighed, "I'm... not sure anymore."

"What do you mean?"

"Mikael was right when he mentioned we were from rival villages. *My* hometown was merely a day's journey farther to the east. Our city-states frequently quarreled over hunting grounds, fishing holes, trade... you name it, Daniel's Holding and Eli's Claim fought over it."

Alyth allowed herself a sheepish grin, "That's how my first meetings with Mikael went. He'd lead his goats along the edge of the forest, I'd shoot warning shots at him to stay away. We'd bicker... or at least *I'd* argue while he teased me. Then about five years ago, I was having a really bad day in the field, and he was leading his herd right at the edge of the forest line like usual. For a moment, I decided I was going to finally shoot one of those damn goats. I notched an arrow... then I saw it out of the corner of my eye. "

Her eyes drifted off into space from the memory. "A cougar, slinking through the tall grasses, no doubt looking for a potential meal from the herd. I hadn't ever seen the big cats that far north before, and the sight enthralled me. So much so that it took Mikael shouting at me wondering what I was waiting for before I took my shot."

He had known both the cougar and I were there. When I asked him why he didn't just scare the animal away, he replied that he didn't want me to return to my town without some meat from my hunt. So not only had he *seen* me from my blind, he could see that my hunting had been fruitless up until that point."

Pirogoeth chirped thoughtfully, "Guess he really *was* that observant before he joined the militia, huh?"

Alyth nodded, "He knew I was from the other town, and he still helped me. He even helped me bind up the kill and carry it back to my cart. It was the damned sweetest thing anyone had ever done for me. I've always been a bit of a tomboy, and claimed I disliked attention from men... but... gosh, even when he does that intentionally awful flirting of his, it's just his little way of saying he cares without actually saying it."

"And punching him or hitting him with whatever happens to be on hand is yours?" Pirogoeth asked.

"He probably thinks so," Alyth snorted.

Then slight smile faded into a worried line, and the marksman said uncertainly, "But lately I've been thinking... you know that entire 'serendipity' thing that I talked about?"

Pirogoeth nodded.

Alyth asked, "Have you ever heard a little voice in your head tell you, 'yes, this is what you should be doing?' That was the feeling I had, pushing me in this scrawny little goat herder's direction. I had always thought of it as two very different people attracting to each other... but when you and Aurora started talking about the Chosen, and how those spirits push you in certain directions..."

Pirogoeth uttered the conclusion, "You're worried that the Chosen spirits pushed the two of you into feelings that you wouldn't normally have."

Alyth let her worry tint her voice. "What if... these 'feelings' I've had aren't really mine? What if I *should* despise this obnoxious, annoying, irritating, cute, adorable, kind... gah! See what I mean?"

Pirogoeth tried to be reassuring, though being rather unsure herself she doubted it would be much. "Well, there's not much we actually know about what even *makes* a person Chosen, much less the nature of the spirits that guide our paths, but there's never been any evidence that they do anything as specific as manipulate specific thoughts or emotions of people. Granted, it wasn't my field of expertise... but once we have peace, I suppose I could pen an appeal to Domina Morgana about any knowledge she might have to cast light on this matter?"

The mage forced herself not to shudder at the thought. While she had never actually *met* the Domina of Tortuga in person, Pirogoeth had enough contact via message, rare telepathic communication, and from second hand sources to know that Morgana was not someone she wanted to exchange much of *anything* with. The Domina had not spared any words in her disdain for Pirogoeth, and the feeling had become mutual fairly quickly.

Alyth shook her head, "I wouldn't ask you to go to such lengths on my account. That's the best answer I could hope for."

"For what it's worth, Goat..."

"*Please* don't call him that while we're alone," Alyth groaned. "It's bad enough he calls himself that Coders-awful name in public and all of you encourage it."

Pirogoeth chuckled, "Very well. *Mikael* has been reliable, faithful, friendly, compassionate, skilled... among all his other positive traits. That he's a little goofy and silly seems like a small price to pay, and personally I can see why you'd find that appealing, even if the two of you had met completely by chance and not by serendipity."

Alyth exhaled heavily. "I'm not good at this sort of talk. Thank you for listening."

Pirogoeth offered a smile. "Don't mention it."

Then the marksman's eyes gleamed dangerously. "Now let's talk about you and our little medic..."

"Let's... not..." Pirogoeth replied nervously, "After all, this is rather silly... don't you think? Two grown women chatting impotently about boys?"

"Nuh uh. You're not slipping away after you got me to spill all my innermost thoughts and feelings."

The mage was mercifully spared by the sounds of the returning teammates from their baths, and Alyth decided cleaning herself was more important than embarrassing Pirogoeth. She stood, and said, "You win... for now..." before leaving the suite.

Alyth was intercepted before she could do so by Goat. The

scout quickly embraced the marksman around her waist and dipped her backwards, Alyth's face turning red with indignation while he smiled teasingly.

"I just want you to know that you have nothing to fear of anyone stealing my affections," he chirped, causing Alyth's scowl to deepen, and with a quick series of movements, pull herself back up by using the collar of his shirt, then throw him to the ground roughly by hooking her right leg around his left and pushing.

She looked down on Goat, and snarled, "You are insufferable." Then the marksman stomped off saying, "Hurry up, everyone. I want to get cleaned up now."

Goat had pushed himself up, leaning back on his elbows. "And you're sure I can't watch?"

"I swear to the Coders, if I catch you peeping on me, I'm going to *kill* you."

In light of Alyth's revelations, Pirogoeth couldn't help but notice how carefully worded that threat was... and how it was also effectively an invitation, because if Goat really didn't want Alyth to see him, she wouldn't, and they both knew that.

He animatedly shrugged his shoulders, "Wouldn't be particularly new anyway. I've already see..."

He was cut off as Alyth threw her quiver at his head.

Pirogoeth ducked back into the suite, and pulled out one of her books for some light reading while she waited for her turn in the springs. As confounding as her affections were, at least she didn't have *that* sort of dynamic. And rather than think about that further, she retreated into her books, where she at least knew what was what.

The mage had more than magic tomes in her satchel. She had a profound interest in history, especially of the ancient empires of times ages ago, and the reason why this mission through Quan'Dor was a trial in maintaining focus on their goal. She also consumed reams of compelling fictional stories from around the world, finding the flights of fancy to be just as engaging and a learning experience as any book of fact.

The bright red covered book that she pulled from her satchel was both of those... if she was willing to be very loose with the definitions of "historical" and "compelling." For example, she highly doubted that elven men had ever been as "strapping and broad in shoulders as a vital bull," or that they had survived until the Avalon of fifty years ago, or that a vital, strapping, elven lord (did they even call themselves "lords" for that matter) would have interest in a "plain farmhand girl" (apparently having a "heaving bosom" twice the size of her waist was "plain" by Avalonian standards).

But she liked the book anyway, if only because it allowed her to live vicariously through characters so woefully underdeveloped that she could pretty much inject herself into the narrative without guilt that she was dismissing the hard work of the author.

Socrato had taught her that no book tells exactly the same story twice. Like most things he said, it was something that she needed time to wrap her mind around to get to the subtle interpretations her master liked to weave into what he thought were clever nuggets of wisdom.

That axiom was even true with something as base as the book in her hands. Each time she read it she learned something new. Like this time, she realized that Bellia loved to play with locks of hair that hung off her right ear when she was nervous. Pirogoeth could picture the girl twisting the strands into knots as Edvaard (she suspected the author slammed a cluster of letters together to come up with that name) approached her.

Edvaard crossed the field far too quickly even for the broad strides Bellia knew he could make with those long, powerfully built legs. But it didn't matter how fast he moved if anyone saw him in broad daylight. "Y... you can't be..."

The protest she tried to finish died under the fiery heat of his mouth as it claimed hers. His tongue felt like it was pouring down her throat, desire dripping down into the very pit of her being. His heat was slowly matched by the heat growing in her core, seducing her to forget her concerns, worries of been seen, and surrendering to Edvaard's obvious sensual need.

But she regained her senses long enough to break content and breathlessly whimper, "But... someone might see you... and if they see you..."

Edvaard growled in annoyance, but accepted her protest long enough to sweep her completely off her feet and sling her over his shoulder while taking his magically entrancing strides towards the hay barn. Over a hundred feet crossed as quickly as Bellia could blink twice, then Edvaard kicking the door open with such force that she was sure the bang would draw the attention of every human within five miles.

31

It was barely another blink before she was rather unceremoniously tossed onto a pile of hay, mercifully covered by a leather tarp because of a leak in the barn's ceiling and the possibility of rain ruining the crop. Not that she got much chance to thank the Coders, or her father for putting that tarp up, before Edvaard was upon her like a hungry wolf, going right for her neck.

Now, with the immediate concerns of discovery abated, Bellia's desire was allowed to rise to meet her partner's. She returned his kisses with those of her own, passionately ripping open his vest to gain access to his finely sculpted chest muscles. But she gasped in indignation when he returned the favor, pushing aside her blouse to violently tear her bodice in half from the front.

"You fiend!" she hissed angrily.

"You did the same to me," he replied, unconcerned by the state of his lover's garments.

"You don't have to return home to people questioning how your clothes got like this!"

"Then you shouldn't have started this game..." Edvaard said with no remorse, instead pushing the rent material away until her chest almost heaved free of the restraining fabric. The elven lord filled his hands with her, kissing the swollen globes repeatedly, but it was merely a diversion from his proper prize, which he wasted no further time claiming. His hand looped into the waistband of her long skirt, dragging it down her smooth legs, baring all he wanted as his head followed downward until it met the junction of her thighs to eagerly take what was his.

Bellia erupted in a lusty moan as contact was made, completely surrendering to the heat that had built up in her belly...

"Ahem!"

Pirogoeth nearly jumped to a full standing position just from her shock alone, slapping her book shut on instinct while breathing heavily and visibly flushed with embarrassment. Alyth had returned from her bath, her hair still damp, and had apparently been trying to get Pirogoeth's attention for some time. "Didn't you hear me calling? It's your turn to clean up."

Her eyes narrowed, then she asked slyly, "What on earth are

you reading?"

"Nothing!" the mage yipped, nervously jamming the book into her satchel. "At least nothing that would interest you! Just some... really engaging arcane study."

Pirogoeth knew that didn't sound the *slightest* bit convincing, and that Alyth didn't buy it. "Arcane study makes you go red in the face like that, does it?" the marksman teased.

"Sometimes... yes..." Pirogoeth answered, wiping her forehead. That wasn't *entirely* a lie. "It can be a very mentally exhausting task. I suppose I didn't realize how deeply I had delved. I apologize."

With all the composure she could muster, Pirogoeth made sure her book was securely tucked in her satchel, and stood up to leave.

Alyth stopped her long enough to toss a gray blanket at her with the advice, "It's not the world's greatest towel, but it'll work, and you'll need it."

Pirogoeth dashed down the steps as quickly as she could, determined not to engage anyone else in conversation lest she display her embarrassment to them as well. She was fairly certain that she almost ran headlong into Wiglaf before the wolf shaman sidestepped her at the last moment, but didn't want to look back to confirm it. It was more important to hit the ground running, which she did, towel flapping behind her as she took with as much speed as she could towards the springs.

It would at least provide an excuse for the color in her face once she ran into Jacques standing guard. He raised an eyebrow at the speed of her appearance, and she waved it off. "I... got distracted to begin with, and didn't want to waste any more of the team's time."

"Thoughtful of you," he replied, jerking his thumb behind him with disinterest. "Don't rush your bath on *my* account though. This might be the last time you get this good of a chance to freshen up for a while. Make it count."

As promised, she had the springs to herself, and as a result she had a surprisingly hard time deciding on which one of the seven pools to choose. She eventually settled on the northeast corner which had a slab of rock jutting upward that almost entirely blocked the view of the spring from anyone on the road.

Even though Jacques had shown no indication that he was looking, Pirogoeth still waded ankle deep into the steadily deepening pool before she began to undress, soaking her trousers in the process as she lifted her legs to pull them off, then tossing them away onto dry land so that they didn't completely fall into the bubbling water. Her gloves then vest followed, then her shirt, then the long process of unbinding her chest wrap.

She spun on a swivel before she took her next steps, wading into water that rose just above her hips, and sighed in dismay. No one else was even within a hundred feet of her and the view completely obstructed, and she was *still* nervous and embarrassed about herself.

The descending water gave her the insulation she needed to focus on cleaning, the burbling blocking out any outside sounds and shrouding her eyes from seeing any play of the moonlight that would convince her that someone was coming. She was finally able to focus on the dirt and grime of days of traveling to wash of her, occasionally with some coaxing from a washcloth.

And how she *didn't* realize someone actually *was* approaching until she heard her name.

"Pirogoeth?"

The mage stumbled at hearing her name, fell backwards, and mercifully hitting the surface of the pool in a fully spread pratfall meant that the softer water broke the bulk of her fall rather than the stone underneath it. She eventually thrashed back to her feet, sputtering water and not looking the slightest bit alluring as she processed that it was Taylor's voice that called out to her.

He had pulled up short at the other side of the natural divider, mercifully offering the mage that barrier while she brushed her hair out of her eyes. "What are you doing here?" She finally demanded after she had regained enough composure to sound properly angry. "How and why did the sergeant let you pass?"

Taylor coughed nervously, and replied, "He... well... he suggested to me that I stop hovering outside and get... this... out of our systems. Whatever it is... we have."

"And what exactly is it that we have?" She asked. She realized that at some point she had crossed her arms over her chest, which made absolutely no sense considering that Taylor couldn't see her from his position.

"A mutual attraction. A heavy tension due to that," the corpsman replied candidly.

Pirogoeth reeled from the admission. Not because she didn't agree, but because he wasn't supposed to be so blunt about it. That was not something her experience with this sort of interaction told her to expect. "Well, I suppose that's *one* way of putting it," the mage mumbled, more to fill the ensuing silence than to offer anything substantial.

"Is there any other way?" Taylor asked, "Would it help if I waxed poetically about your mystical allure? Or of your magic that means more than the spells that come with such ease from your fingers? What of the radiance of your smile? Or the sweet song of the words that come from your lips?"

"No..." she admitted sheepishly, "but... I like hearing it nonetheless."

She was rewarded with that light, musical laugh that she had come to enjoy, and it brought a rare smile to her face. Gulping down her nerves, Pirogoeth decided Taylor wasn't the only one who could cut straight to the point. "So, if Jacques told you to come in here to relieve our tension... why haven't you?"

"There's a story I never told you," Taylor answered, "And it's pertinent to your question."

Pirogoeth didn't reply audibly initially until she remembered that they couldn't see each other. "Oh!" she yelped when she pieced together that he wouldn't be able to pick up on the silent cue. "Please, go on."

"I've pushed myself on more than one woman. Not intentionally, but my interest was so overbearing that it coerced positive responses that they probably would not have wanted to give at that time. One such example was of a woman in in a town called Terrasa. I thought I had earned the affections of a cute little chimera girl... just the cutest little floppy dog ears... chimeras weren't normally my thing, but this girl seemed positively enchanting."

Like my life in Avalon, however, I was much more enamored in her than she was in me. I found myself in the grasp of a very large, very angry bear woman, and I wound up discovering just how much force was needed to toss a man through a window. For the record... it takes a surprisingly large amount. Window glass doesn't shatter nearly as easily as you might think."

Pirogoeth giggled at the image, even though at the time it could not have been something Taylor took lightly.

"I meant what I said earlier when we were all teasing you," he explained. "I'm not going to assume any consent. I'm only going to go where I'm invited."

The mage smiled, then said warmly, "Well, then consider yourself invited, dear sir."

She heard the rustling of clothing being discarded, and bit her lower lip in anticipation as the corpsman finally rounded the rocky divider and into her view. He didn't have shoulders like a bull or bulging biceps, but the life of a militiaman certainly did him *some* favors. He was certainly in good shape, with a very defined muscle structure.

The mage's eyes drifted downward in further assessment. *Very* well defined. She had seen more than one sculpture in Aramathea that could have used Taylor's inspiration.

The corpsman slowly waded into the water, and Pirogoeth became acutely aware that the water that was up to her waist was about up to Taylor's mid-thigh. Not that it was necessarily a *problem*, as it meant she had a splendid view, but it also made her feel very small, and far more vulnerable than she would have liked.

Taylor helped assuage those fears by gently taking her arms and pulling them away from her chest, then tilting her chin up to look him in the eyes. "Don't ever show shame. Don't let anyone tell you you're anything but lovely."

She would have nodded if he hadn't stolen the opportunity by covering her lips with his. Her arms moved of their own volition as they wrapped around his neck, and she became so lost in the contact that she wasn't even perturbed by her center of balance shifting as he leaned her backward to the point that he was the only thing keeping her from an unsightly dunk in the spring.

Pirogoeth hadn't thought "getting swept off her feet" really had a literal interpretation, nor "feeling like she was walking on air" when describing a romantic affection. But right now? Gravity could go whistle.

Taylor spun her about, the movement momentarily making her break lip contact as he gently lowered her onto the edge of the pool, the surprisingly cool rock contrasting the heat on her skin. She reached out to him, only to find nothing but air. Taylor had slowly slid down her body, kissing her breasts, navel, then right down between her legs.

Pirogoeth's squeak was *nothing* like a lusty moan, and she flushed with embarrassment at such a reaction. But at the same time, the sensation wasn't as advertised either. This... wasn't particularly pleasant. The only conclusion the mage could really reach was that a tongue really shouldn't go *there*.

If she showed any displeasure, Taylor didn't get the hint, but he at least returned to her mouth, which she should have found more welcome, except for that growing clammy sensation growing in her stomach that should have been the promised wanton heat from sexual activity. By the time Taylor had actually gotten to the heart of the matter, Pirogoeth had lost any and all passion she started with.

This is disgusting. Stop this right now!

The mage's eyes flared in dismay, understanding just what was happening. Why was her Chosen spirit imposing itself *now?*

Whether fortunately or no, Pirogoeth didn't need to take any initiative to end the tryst. Taylor caught Pirogoeth's expression, saw whatever magic should have been there wasn't, and pulled away with a forlorn growl of "Damn it."

He swiftly stepped around her as Pirogoeth frantically tried to scramble to her feet in chase, a task that the wet rock and her current position did not make easy. "Taylor! Wait! It's not you... it's..."

"Like hell it isn't me," the corpsman replied. "I know damn well what it is. It's what I've been chasing ever since my wife died, and if I'm honest, even before that. You're just the latest in a line of conquests, conquests of an old man trying to relive his younger days."

"I'm *not* a child!" Pirogoeth hissed, her distress turning towards annoyance.

"Yeah you are. Whether you like it or not, and I just took something from you that you can never get back."

Taylor had dressed so quickly that he was heading back to camp before Pirogoeth had even managed to grab her wrap, and she screamed in frustration at his retreating form. That got Jacques attention, long enough for him to receive some curt words from the corpsman. Beyond that, Jacques wasn't going to leave his post, and was powerless to keep Taylor from going anywhere.

The mage didn't even bother with the wrap, leaving it for the ghosts of the elven people as she threw on the rest of her clothes and stomped off angrily after her quarry. She brushed off Jacques's concern with a withering glare, and gave him no further answers as she continued her pursuit.

Goat imposed himself as she reached the party's floor in the tree dwelling. "So, did you have fun? Get nice and clean, or nice and dirty *then* clean?"

Apparently, the scowl she gave him wasn't any more telling than the scowls she usually gave him when he was being obnoxious, because he only needled further.

"Oh. Didn't even bother getting the clean part? Or the dirty part?"

At *that* point, the scout began to sense something had gone very wrong. He looked over to his room, where Taylor had no doubt hidden himself, and shouted, "Okay... why'd you break the mage?"

Finally, Pirogoeth had enough, and lashed out, picking Goat up by the collar of his shirt through nothing but raw mental force and throwing him roughly into the wall. There was a small part of her that regretted the sound the back of his head made as it whip-lashed against the wall, and she would probably regret it more later, but her anger was momentarily in control.

She resolutely stomped over to the other suite, ignoring Goat's pained groan that he couldn't feel his fingers, and nearly pounced at the first person she saw.

Aurora. And no Taylor in sight.

"Where is he?" Pirogoeth demanded sternly.

"Who? Taylor?" Aurora asked, then shook her head. "I don't know. He hasn't come this way."

"But Goat..."

"Was being an ass," Alyth interjected from the common room, then to the scout she grumbled, "Oh shut up, you deserved it."

Part of her wanted to tear the entire Underground Empire apart until she found the bastard, but another decided it was simply better to bide her time. He had to come back eventually.

Pirogoeth sulked back into the common room, ignored Alyth's questions, slunk into her suite, gathered up her satchel, pack, and sleeping bag, then retreated to another another room on the floor. "If anyone needs me, I'll be in here," the mage snarled. "I can't promise I'll answer, though."

At that point, she slammed the door shut, threw her gear down in the middle of the floor, and where all the anger abruptly melted into shame. She flopped stomach down onto the sleeping bag, trying not to cry... or at least not cry audibly enough that anyone would be able to hear her. Why was it such a problem to... enjoy herself? Why did her damn Chosen spirit have to ruin everything? Taylor probably hated her and thought she was a terrible tease.

Someone knocked on her door, and she wanted to ignore it. She *wanted* to curl up into a little ball and die. But she doubted either was going to be a real option.

"Pirogoeth. Open up," Jacques ordered. "We need to talk."

He didn't sound angry, or even disappointed, but his tone of voice still suggested that declining was not going to be acceptable.

"If you don't open this door yourself, Aurora here is going to open it *for* you."

"No, I am not," the healer assured. "She'll speak to us when she is ready."

Pirogoeth groaned in resignation, pulling herself to her feet, and triggering the door lock for Jacques and Aurora, and promptly shut it behind them. While she didn't have much choice to address the team leader, that didn't mean that she wanted to encourage any other visitors or eavesdroppers. She sat down on her knees back on her sleeping bag, if for no reason than she wanted to at least be able to look Jacques in the eye when he sat down cross legged in front of her, Aurora doing the same directly to Pirogoeth's right.

"Sorry it took so long," Jacques said, "But I wanted to hunt down Taylor before I talked to you."

Aurora gave Pirogoeth a hug, and added, "I've never seen you so upset before, what happened? What did he do?"

"*He* didn't do anything wrong," Pirogoeth insisted, "It was *me*. My Chosen spirit apparently didn't approve of Taylor's affections."

"Then why were you so angry with him?" Jacques asked.

"Because he wasn't listening to me!" Pirogoeth asserted. "Called me a child and that he took something precious and just being a general obnoxious prat."

Aurora asked Jacques, "What did Taylor have to say?"

"To be honest, I didn't give him much chance to say anything," Jacques replied. "I was too busy yelling at him for wandering off alone and potentially getting himself killed. From what I overheard of the conversation the two had, Pirogoeth's explanation matches what I heard."

He turned his focus back on Pirogoeth, and said, "The only thing that I want to know right now is if Taylor's going to be a problem for you. Because I'll turn him loose right now and tell him to find his own way out of this hole and not even give him the courtesy of a look back."

Jacques was furious at Taylor for some reason, and *not* just because the corpsman went off on his own. Perhaps there was more to Jacques and Taylor's discussion than the sergeant was letting on. "What *really* happened between you and Taylor... sir?"

"That's between him and me," Jacques replied. "I need to know if you and him will be a problem going forward."

Pirogoeth shook her head animatedly, "No. For Coder's sake, *no*. Provided he's actually willing to talk to me once in a while without getting all guilty."

The sergeant smiled, a very awkward expression for him, and patted the mage's shoulder. "Well, if it ever does, just tell me." Then to Aurora, he asked, "Does that settle your concerns, Aurora?"

39

The healer bit her lower lip, and admitted, "I... don't know... honestly. *My* Chosen spirit wanted me to be here, and I'm not entirely certain why."

Pirogoeth's fugue instantly snapped to that confession. Why would Aurora's Chosen spirit be interested in any of this? What did it have to do with anything?

"Is it saying or suggesting anything now?" Jacques pressed.

Aurora shook her head in response. "No."

Jacques stood, and absentmindedly brushed off his knees for no real reason. "Then I'm going to consider this matter closed for the moment. You can go ahead and spend the night here, Pirogoeth. Take the night to decompress and have some time to yourself."

"But what about the people in my suite?" the mage asked.

"Oh, I have something in mind. You just relax, okay?"

"But..."

Aurora shushed her with another hug before standing. "Let the sergeant handle it, okay?"

Pirogoeth exhaled in defeat. They weren't going to budge no matter how much Pirogoeth protested, and she had to admit that she didn't terribly want to have to be around the others right at that moment anyway. "Very well, I'll see you in the morning."

Aurora let herself and Jacques out, graciously closing the door behind them. Pirogoeth slumped down onto her sleeping bag, peeking out over her arms to see the open end of her satchel, and that damn red cover book that she had taken such a base liking to. The mage pulled it out, threw it across the room, and set it on fire for good measure.

Sleep didn't come easily or quickly, especially as her mind starting twisting around the Chosen spirit's role in the events of today. It reminded her of her discussion with Alyth, and how wrong she had had been in her assurances.

Just how deep did the Chosen influence go?

Did she even want to know the answer?

~   ~   ~   ~   ~

Pirogoeth got enough sleep by the time Jacques made the call to break camp that she wasn't one of the walking dead, at least. She stumbled out of her room after gathering up her gear, then learned just what Jacques' plan had been.

The sergeant jerked his finger at the suite the mage had vacated, and said, "I suggest you let them out quick."

"Yes please," Alyth called out from the other side of the door.

Pirogoeth's eyes bulged in worry, and she crossed the distance in three hasty strides, her hand crackling with the magic to unlock the door before her feet had even set. That proved to be for the best, as her momentum took her past the door as it opened and out of the way when Tyronica and Alyth barreled past in their haste down the stairs.

She opened her mouth to ask what that was about, when Taylor's voice answered without prompting.

"They've been locked in there with me all day, and there wasn't a toilet in the suite surprisingly," the corpsman said flatly. "Tyronica swore that if she had no other choice, she was going to go right on my face. Alyth offered to hold me down. I have a good many kinks, but I can safely say that is *not* one of them."

Pirogoeth could feel the chill in the air, even if it was just imagined. She now understood just what Jacques' plan had been, and jumped to try and defuse any animosity. "Taylor, I *swear* I had nothing to do with... that."

"I know you didn't," he replied.

She dropped her head, and added, "Please understand last night was *my* fault."

"It was *both* of us," Taylor corrected. "It's not like I was coerced. We started... something changed... and we stopped. It doesn't matter what that reason is. You didn't want it anymore, and I had to stop, no matter how much desire I had to continue. I should have been more observant, and that was *my* fault."

"So... you don't hate me?"

Taylor flashed a smile that gave some warmth to the chill. "Hardly. If I hated every girl that decided they didn't want my affection, I dare say I'd despise nearly half the continent."

"So... then friends still? More?"

He patted her affectionately on the top of her head. "Let's just start with friends, and see what happens from there, okay, 'Ro?"

Her eyes narrowed in annoyance, and she grumbled, "Is 'Pirogoeth' really *that* hard for you people to say?"

The corpsman's response was a quiet chuckle, and the mage clenched her teeth before falling in behind him. Jacques was no doubt want to be on the move as soon as possible, and it would probably do her good to actually be ready to go after all the drama of last night.

Chapter Three: Odd Angles

"And you're sure this is it?" Jacques asked.

"Well, I won't be absolutely sure until we get closer," Aurora amended, "But this is the strongest the flow of magic has felt so far."

The city in the horizon certainly *looked* the part of an imperial capital. It was at least twice as large as the other cities they had passed through, and where the previous towns had spiraled off of one central dwelling, this city looked more like a forest of stone, with several large elven dwellings lording over smaller ones.

There were also many more roads winding into the city than in any of the previous, at least twelve from what Pirogoeth could see, and no doubt several more on the other side that were blocked from view. This was it. If not the actual elven capital, it was almost certainly a hub where Pirogoeth could work her magic.

"Even I can feel it at this point," the mage declared. "Once we find where the power gathers here, it should be enough."

Jacques gestured ahead, and ordered, "Then forward march, folks. You know the drill... let's get this done by morning."

But it became clear that the city's "canopy" was hiding things that would make getting the job done *at all* a trial, much less by the morning.

Goat saw it first, pointing upwards as the team crossed underneath the smaller dwellings that marked the city limits. "Anyone with arachnophobia probably shouldn't look up," the scout said in such a way that of course encouraged everyone, fear of spiders or not, to do exactly that.

The underside of the stone leaves were interlaced with silken strands of spider webbing, to the point that it looked more silken than stone. In that distance, hundreds of the spider-bull chimeras wound through the networks of webbing, seemingly unconcerned by the team below... at least for now.

"Oh, Coders no..." Tyronica mumbled, forcing herself to stare at the ground.

Pirogoeth pondered on what she was seeing, despite being of Tyronica's mind, "I wonder if the ambient lighting here is so bright that even though it's 'night' above that they're still active..."

"Did any of the Bullders we saw before show any proclivity to web building?" Alyth asked.

"No *spidull* showed those tendencies," Goat both confirmed

and corrected.

Tyronica grumbled, "Silence. These are nopebeasts, forged from hells no, and hailing from the lands of nuh uh."

"Scared of some spiders?" Wiglaf snorted.

"Live with a spider chimera sometime, Dayne," Jacques grumbled. "You'll gain a completely healthy fear of them quickly enough. I can't imagine these beasts will be any less temperamental or deadly if provoked either."

"You mean like right now?" Pirogoeth asked, pointing to where the chimeric beasts had now definitely taken an interest in the party, descending from the canopy with their spindly legs wrapped around thick silk strands. The chimeras descended far faster than their size should have allowed, mere seconds after Pirogoeth's warning before hundreds had reached the ground level.

Jacques didn't waste time ordering Aurora, pointing to a mercifully nearby door of a smaller building, "Aurora! Get that door open! Pirogoeth, give us some space!"

That proved to be fortunate, as the spidulls (Pirogoeth found that the easier name to wrap around, with apologies to Alyth), didn't waste time launching on the attack. The mage intercepted the first wave with a ring of fire, but the flames died too quickly for the team to completely retreat, giving five spidulls an opening at the retreating humans.

Wiglaf provided additional distraction, quickly identifying one weakness of their foe as he swept low to crush the front two legs of the nearest foe, causing the chimeric beast to stumble and crash into the side of the dwelling, it's still intact legs flailing as it tried to regain its balance. The wolf shaman quickly identified that it would pose no immediate threat, giving him time to sidestep a stabbing leg from a second attacker then cut out three legs on its right flank.

Alyth tried to give him an opening to retreat, thudding an arrow square in the chest of a flanking spidull, but it seemed the upper body of the creatures were much more resilient than the legs. The beast barely winced from what by all rights should have been a kill shot, then demonstrated that while their legs might be fragile they were still dangerous, puncturing Wiglaf's hide armor and left shoulder straight through and out five inches.

Wiglaf roared in response, snapped the offending leg off, then managed to swing his cudgel about with enough force from his right hand alone to snap the horns and neck of his attacker. And while adrenaline was carrying the Dayne for now, Pirogoeth knew that wasn't going to last forever.

She jumped outside momentarily to set another encroaching spidull ablaze, then as it tumbled past into an incendiary demise the mage ignited a third fire wall in a semi-circle that would give Wiglaf enough time to retreat. To reinforce the point, she screamed, "Get in here before you get yourself killed!"

He complied, reluctantly, even with a damn spider leg embedded with his shoulder he entertained jumping through the flames to continue the fight. He jumped through the doorway seconds before the flames died enough for the spidulls to continue advancing, and just in time for Pirogoeth to seal the door before the chimeras could get more than one leg crushed by the stone door as it slapped shut.

Tyronica found herself transfixed by the still quivering, razor sharp appendage while Pirogoeth and Aurora started on treatment for Wiglaf. That was easier than either anticipated, as the adrenaline induced rage had quickly drained away and the Dayne had turned white as a ghost. He fell to his knees, eyes glazed off into space, as Aurora valiantly tried to keep his bulk from dropping face first to the floor.

"Tyronica!" Pirogoeth ordered, catching the Aramathean's attention. "Hold him for us, please." She then snapped her fingers at Goat, and said, "You pull out the leg when we tell you. Taylor, apply pressure to the back of the wound, because it's probably going to bleed like a fountain until we can patch up the damage. Aurora, you start healing the wound the instant you can, I'll cleanse for any poison and disease while you're doing it."

"Presuming these beasts have any sort of poison or contaminant that your magics can purge," Goat noted.

"Trying not to think about that, thank you," Pirogoeth grumbled with annoyance. "Now, everyone ready? Pull it out, Goat."

The scout gripped the broken spidull leg from the front side, and fell over on his backside when he found it took surprisingly little force to pull it free. Taylor, on the other hand, was ready for exactly what came, having double padded gauze on the wound as the first layer instantly stained crimson.

Pirogoeth was honestly a bit surprised, and even proud, at how perfectly their motley little band worked as a team. Wiglaf lost surprisingly little blood considering, and was already starting to regain the color to his skin. As his breathing steadied, Pirogoeth instructed Tyronica to lay him down to rest, and then she processed their situation.

Interestingly enough, the spidulls weren't trying to get inside the dwelling. "They made a few experimental tests of the windows and doors while you were healing Wiglaf, but otherwise gave up quickly enough," Jacques said. "Whether that means they're so dumb that we're no longer interesting, or smart enough to know that we can't stay in here forever..." he then shrugged for effect.

"Do you think you can scry our destination from here?" Aurora asked Pirogoeth.

"If you all think we'd be secure here for several hours, I could try." Pirogoeth replied.

Jacques looked through the window, assessing the scene outside, then said, "Might as well give it a shot. We've got some time to kill while Wiglaf rests up anyway."

The mage exhaled sharply. She had a sinking suspicion how this would go, but felt she owed it to the team to try.

Finding her center was a tricky thing in perfectly normal conditions. As she closed her eyes this time, the only thing she could manage was to hear her still thudding heart in her chest. She tried very hard not to think about the last time she successfully scryed being by accident after she had fallen asleep. She tried to force herself to calm down, which predictably had the exact opposite effect.

Then she heard the scratching again, this time from above, and it startled her out of the beginnings of whatever trance she could achieve. At the same time, Jacques jumped back from the window, spidull legs again scratching against the glass, even if they weren't showing any effectiveness about getting inside.

"Coders, whatever you're doing, Pirogoeth... stop!" the former pirate yelled.

Pirogoeth wasn't sure she had heard a more welcome order since she joined the militia.

"It would seem that the monsters can sense arcane energy usage, and are drawn aggressively to it." Aurora observed.

"That would make sense if they were created and bred as defenders against human encroachment," Pirogoeth agreed.

"Then clearly the answer is to toss the mage outside and wait until the beasts are done picking her bones clean," Wiglaf grumbled weakly. After a beat where the rest of the team stared him down with disgust, he added, "That was... mostly... in jest."

Pirogoeth was the only one who laughed at that, a tired one that reflected her relief. "How are you feeling?"

"Sore," the Dayne replied simply. "Which I suppose is better than dead."

Tyronica helped the shaman sit up, though the motion drained what color had been returning. He wobbled, but declined any concern and refused to lay back down. "So scrying our destination is out of the question then?"

"Unless you want to fight off the eighth level of hell," Jacques replied, "then yes."

"Seventh," Pirogoeth corrected.

"What?"

"The Den of the Spider God was the *seventh* level of Hieri's vision of hell," the mage explained. "The *eighth* level was the Den of the Giant King."

Jacques rolled his eyes and grumbled, "Whatever..."

"Then what *is* our plan?" Tyronica asked. "Wiglaf, would you be able to suggest a direction?"

"The only reason I found the way to Mirror Lake was because I had an intimate knowledge of the area. I have never been to Vazmeade, I only know *of* the settlement."

"Could there be other hubs for Pirogoeth to scry from?" Alyth wondered.

"Possibly," the mage answered. "It's also possible that the closer we get to Vazmeade that I wouldn't *need* to scry deep enough to find it."

Jacques stared back out the window, and grumbled, "Which is all well and good *after* we find a way to get out of here. Because something tells me that hornet's nest we kicked isn't going to quiet down any time soon, so we're going to need a plan."

Pirogoeth pointed to a stairwell in the southwest corner, and said, "Perhaps we can get a better lay of the land up there?"

Jacques nodded, then pointed to the scout. "Goat, you're with us. Everyone else... sit tight."

Even for a smaller building, it had a surprising number of floors. By the time they reached the seventh, the windows there provided a far better view of the surrounding area than any of them could have hoped for, despite the fact that the spidulls had decided to perch on the top of the dwelling and on the stone leaves of the branches.

And where Goat spied a potential avenue for their retreat.

He pointed off between the trunks of two larger buildings to the north-northeast, where what looked like a segment of a massive stone wall stood in the distance. But what was important was that he pointed up. "There's a break in the canopy there," the scout said. "At the very least, we'd have a breather from being attacked from above."

"It's as good of a starting point as any," Jacques decided. "Good work."

Then the sound of a slamming door from the floor below, followed by resounding thuds, got their attention, and sent them scampering down the steps, fearing they would have to fight off spidull attackers far sooner than expected. Instead, Alyth pointed them to a western room of the ground floor, where Wiglaf and Tyronica were putting all their weight onto what looked to be a trap door... a door that was nonetheless bucking an inch with repetitive force from below.

"Wiglaf!" Pirogoeth shrieked, worried that the Dayne was moving about too soon.

"Aurora... hastened my recovery, Despite my protests," he admitted. "Which was fortunate, as our quick-thinking corporal decided *not* to stay put as ordered."

"I saw the door to the cellar... and thought there might be some underground connections," Alyth explained. "I didn't think it would do any harm to find out."

"And then...?" Jacques needled.

"I... discovered that trolls *aren't* extinct on the continent?"

Jacques eyes flared. "That's a *troll* down there?"

"I think so. I didn't get much chance to look before it lunged at me. I don't even know where it came from."

Pirogoeth came to Alyth's defense. "Trolls can literally turn to stone lacking anything to hunt, and reanimate when it senses new prey. Alyth wouldn't have even noticed anything outside of a very large rock. It's amazing she's still alive."

"That's all well and good, but now we're in the middle of a literal rock and a hard place," Jacques replied.

That much was true, the troll from below was pounding on the cellar door with increasing force, to the point that even the abnormally solid elven stone was showing visible cracks. They weren't going to have much time to decide whether they wanted to be killed by the spidulls, or a troll.

"It's only one troll," Goat said. "Think we can kill it?"

"Possibly..." Pirogoeth said, her eyes drifting between the cellar door and the door leading outside. "But I have a better idea..."

She pointed to the outside door and ordered, "Alyth, get ready to open that door when I say." She herself got into position directly in front of that door while issuing the rest. "Wiglaf, Tyronica, open the cellar at the same time. Everyone else, get down, cover your eyes, then follow Jacques when I call for you. You know where we need to be

47

going, right, Goat?"

Goat tapped his forehead and replied, "Yep! Got it right in my old noggin' here."

"Good," Pirogoeth confirmed, biting her lower lip as she prepared herself for her unvoiced part in the plan. She knew exactly what she needed to do, and what book she was going to offer up as a sacrifice, but it was going to be *really* risky. Too slow, and she no doubt gets trampled by a troll. Too quick, and she'd be out in no man's land with spidulls all looking for a tasty arcane morsel.

"What are you planning, Pirogoeth?" Jacques asked.

"Just run. You'll know when. It'd take too much time to explain fully," the mage answered. Taking a deep breath, she barked, *"Now! Open them!"*

Wiglaf and Tyronica rolled in separate directions while Goat whipped open the front door. Pirogoeth scampered backward into the city proper, momentarily amazed with herself that she didn't stumble and fall, casting an immolation spell on the troll as it predictably smashed through the cellar, focusing immediately on Pirogoeth.

While fire was one of the secrets to killing a troll, that was only after the beast had taken considerable damage, and its hide split where the more delicate flesh could be burned. Otherwise, the only thing that setting a troll on fire accomplished was to make it incredibly angry and smell incredibly bad. The smell could be ignored... but the charging troll, its deformed jaw opening in a roar to display a veritable gallery of shattered obsidian teeth, couldn't be.

And that was when she sacrificed the book she had chosen, throwing it at the troll and then targeting it with a disintegration spell. This, under any other circumstance, would be considered insane. Even the weakest magical tomes stored very large amounts of energy, and destroying a tome released all that energy in one burst.

This... was an unusual circumstance, one that required an insane solution.

Despite that, the eruption of brilliant white light as the tome vaporized was too diffused to do any fatal damage to the troll. Not that she wanted it to. It was that flash of light that she was going for, a flash so intense that she could see the bones beneath her forearm as she covered her eyes. It had been damn near blinding, and she was prepared for it. For the troll, and the spidulls swarming from all sides, they had no chance.

The troll stumbled past her, crashing into a spidull that had been stalking Pirogoeth from behind. That sparked a melee between the two, quickly drawing in nearby spidulls that were stumbling to find *something* to attack. It was a conflict that didn't promise to end soon... even the knife like front legs of the spidulls had trouble puncturing the troll's hide, and the spidull's numbers kept the troll occupied.

"Run for it!" Pirogoeth screeched to her teammates, hoping they hadn't been stupid and watched the explosion. "Now!"

Mercifully, the team emerged with enough sight to follow Goat and Jacques who had taken the lead. "What in the black pits was *that*, Pirogoeth?" Tyronica asked as the mage joined the procession.

Pirogoeth summarized bluntly, "Destroyed a tome. Released the energy inside. Good distraction."

"*What* tome?"

"Just some silly one that Dominus Socrato gave me. Blaine's Illusions. I tried to leave it in Kartage, but he insisted I take it. There was literally nothing of value in it, even if I was particularly skilled at illusion magic. Stuff like how to pretend to be inside a glass box for a week."

The banter died off, because while the distraction had been remarkably good, it didn't blind and misdirect every spidull in the city. There was more than enough of a mob that the team had to outrun as they make their break, slowing the pursuit with walls of fire and well placed arrows. While Alyth found that arrows to the chimeric beast's chests did little, shooting them in the abdomen was much more effective.

It was vital in keeping off pressure from above, as those shots caused the spidulls to lose focus on their descent, disrupting their silk production and resulting in fatal falls to the road below.

"These beasts truly are not that tough," Wiglaf grunted as one hit the road ahead of him, its neck audibly snapping as it crunched headfirst into the stone.

"We're the ones running, aren't we?" Aurora reminded.

Wiglaf grunted in response and went silent.

The team's hurried retreat showed them two very important things they didn't realize at the start. Firstly, that their destination was a *lot* bigger than it seemed at first glance. Secondly, that meant it was a lot farther away then they first thought.

Goat stopped abruptly, prompting Alyth to crash into him, the rest of the party stumbling to each side to prevent further collisions.

"Why the hells are you stopping for?" the marksman demanded angrily.

Goat answered with a smirk, "The spidulls stopped pursuing

us."

That much was true. They had reached the break in the stone canopy, and learned how it came to be.

It was no doubt destroyed with the rest of surrounding area.

They had been so used to seeing the remarkable resilience of the abandoned elven empire that it was jarring to find actual ruins. But the land around them looked almost like it had been stomped flat, the staunch tree dwelling toppled and pounded into rubble.

"Ya know, I'm starting to think we shouldn't be here," Goat commented.

Tyronica countered, "You'd rather go back into that chimeric hell?"

"They stopped chasing us for a *reason*. And I'd rather not learn in the worst possible way that the reason for that, and the reason for this, are connected."

The Aramathean soldier really didn't know what to say to that. Pirogoeth didn't fault her for that. The mage really didn't want to consider it either.

Segments of the road were so buried by the ruins that it was fortunate the spidulls had stopped their pursuit because of the time it took to traverse the blockages.

Due to the delays, it was nearly "night" by the time they finally reached their destination, a distinct difference due to the ruins not being able to provide the same light that the rest of the city did. The details began to stand out from that perspective.

It wasn't exactly a wall, it was some sort of stadium judging from the curve of its construction enclosing a large center space... or at least did at one time. While said stadium was still standing, it had taken a tremendous amount of damage; must of the western side had been ripped down with what appeared to be tremendous force, considering how chunks of stone clearly from the stadium wall had crashed down nearly a half mile from where they had once stood.

"Part of me really doesn't want to know how that happened," Goat quipped. "Another part of me is terrified we're gonna find out."

"Probably something as long dead as the rest of the elves," Jacques snarled, glaring angrily at the scout. "And not worth trying to give us a scare in a situation which is plenty scary enough."

Pirogoeth saw right through that attempt, and she suspected the rest of the team did as well. The spidulls wouldn't be too scared to continue their hunt over some long passed threat. Whatever was lurking in these ruins had been here recently enough for it to be fresh in the memory.

"Well... then you're really not going to like this, sir..." Aurora said sheepishly. "But the hub for all the flow of energy here... it's inside."

"You have *got* to be kidding me..." Jacques grumbled, dropping his face into his palm.

"It's a prime opportunity," Pirogoeth noted, "It's at least worth checking out."

The former pirate sighed, and relented. "I suppose the attempt is worth not stumbling blindly through the underground. Let's go..."

They took advantage of the opened west side rather than try to navigate whatever halls might exist on the stadium's exterior ring. Pirogoeth had seen arenas before in Grand Aramathea, but nothing of such scale. The interior courtyard alone had to be at least three hundred feet from end to end, if not more.

In a curious change of design, the interior walls were *not* circular, but were six oddly-angled walls forming an extremely irregular hexagram. The two longest walls were to the north and south sides, followed by three shorter walls that formed the eastern side. Finally, the broken down western section would have formed the shortest wall. At the top of those walls, mithril steel lights cast remarkably strong light down onto the courtyard, so strong that night turned to day.

In front of them, a diamond shape had been made out of lighter stone, each corner marked with what must have been shimmering crystal at one time. In the center of the diamond, a raised mound of stone scattered with scattered pieces of crystal signified some sort of importance, but Pirogoeth had no idea what that importance could have been.

"What do you suppose the elves did here?" Alyth wondered out loud.

"Some sort of sport, I'd imagine," Pirogoeth answered. "Though what little scraps of their culture we know didn't mention anything like this."

Aurora had found a long, narrow, smooth club made out of what looked like silver, though couldn't possibly have been considering the ease in which she picked it up to examine it. "I wonder if this was important..."

Goat pointed out past the diamond and said, "I think it's more important that we find out what did *that*, and be anywhere else if it comes back this way."

The scout was referring to a long three-clawed gouge out of the darker stone, the largest of many such scratches that littered the courtyard.

"Pirogoeth... hurry up and do your thing," Jacques ordered.

The mage's eyebrows raised and she said, "My 'thing' could take..."

"I don't *care*. Just *do it*, as quickly as you can."

Pirogoeth bit her tongue, resigned herself to an indignant huff, and marched forward towards the mound in the diamond's center. It seemed like as good of a place as any. She got a good look at what turned out to be a mounting for what must have been a tremendously large object, far larger than the small pieces of translucent white crystal remaining accounted for.

Someone had taken it. But who? And where? And why?

"Anytime, PFC," Jacques grumbled, invoking her rank in a not at all subtle reminder of his authority. He didn't want to be here. To be fair, Pirogoeth didn't think *anybody* on the team wanted to be here. She probably shouldn't want to be here, either. But here, where the magical power of the elves seemed to converge, all she wanted was to peel back the layers of history, and learn everything there was to know of these magical beings, and what happened to them.

Maybe... she'd learn something through scrying.

By happenstance, of course.

She *did* have a primary task, after all.

Pirogoeth crossed her legs around the empty mounting, dropping the black book in her lap. It was much easier to find her center without the immediate spidull threat, though still not easy. The fear of the unknown peril that might or might not be lurking nearby kept her heart rate far too high for a seamless transition into the metaphysical.

But she did it... haltingly... irritatingly... as the artificial Code of the World fashioned by the elves was even less receptive to her intrusion than the natural variant. But she knew too many of the tricks of scrying to be denied at this point. Persistence and stamina paid off, and she immersed herself into the current, her consciousness slowly spreading through the magical network...

At least... until she was abruptly ripped from it in a most unsafe manner.

She wasn't aware that she had screamed until she finally heard Jacques's voice demand with an angry hiss, "Coders, will someone shut her up before that damn thing decides we're worth the trouble?"

She was back in the material world, with a headache so intense that she couldn't even feel her extremities. Her head throbbed with fiery pain alternating with an electric agony.

"Well, you rather *did* literally tear her away from her scrying. I can only imagine she wanted us to use the mint trigger for a *reason*," Taylor chided.

"We didn't have *time* for her to wake up, damnit! Hurry up and gag her or something!"

She became vaguely aware of a cotton-like fabric filling her mouth. Was she still screaming?

"Even I could see the magic energy ripping. I can't imagine that it was healthy."

Magic... ripping? How could Taylor "see" it? She never saw anything during the times she witnessed Socrato scrying, and no one who had witnessed her doing so had ever commented on any visual energy.

"We *all* saw it," Alyth added. "But the sergeant was right. We didn't have time."

"At least we know she's still alive," Wiglaf grumbled in annoyance.

"If this is what you want to call it," Taylor replied. "For all we know her mind is gone."

"And that is different from normal... how?"

Finally Pirogoeth had enough control of her own body to spit out the makeshift gag and snarl weakly, "Do the world a favor and jump into a volcano, Dayne."

Her sight started clearing, and saw Aurora hovering over her, tears dropping liberally. "I couldn't heal you... your mind was so stretched..."

"Forcibly breaking a scry is dangerous," Pirogoeth grumbled. "It could have killed me. My spirit wasn't fully in my body. The majority of it was channeled through..."

Pirogoeth lunged forward, groaning as the world spun and her head throbbed painfully again. Pushing away Aurora's concern, she looked for her black tome. It wasn't in her satchel. It wasn't in her lap, nor did she she it anywhere nearby.

The mage's voice turned dark as she slowly demanded, "Where... is my tome?"

Jacques helped her to her feet, and Pirogoeth processed that they were in one of the interior stadium halls on the lower level. She was vaguely aware of what looked like empty booths and merchant stands along the perimeter while Jacques marched her over to a tunnel that led to the courtyard.

He then pointed out into the courtyard, and said, "Over there. Have fun."

Pirogoeth found her tome easily enough. It was in fact glowing with a ghostly white energy, phantom wisps curling around the massive talon capped paws of a rock dragon. It's stone scaled, diamond shaped head rested on top of those paws, giving all the impression of a sleeping beast, though if she remembered the tales of these great wyrms correctly, such appearances meant little.

Jacques mistook her expression as he said, "If you think you're surprised, imagine how all of us reacted when we saw it drop down from the ceiling of the cavern."

Pirogoeth shook her head, both to negate Jacques's assumption and to help clear her mind from the remaining fog settled over it. "Not terribly surprised, honestly. Dragons could live thousands of years with a sufficient food supply, which I suspect the spidulls fill nicely. I'm trying to figure out how I'm going to get my tome back."

"Get it *back*?" Jacques scoffed. "Are you insane?"

"Without that tome, fighting the Winter Walkers would be the height of insanity... perhaps even more so than fighting a dragon."

"You don't even know how to properly use it, girl."

"I know that the Winter Walkers fear whatever it can do. That's enough. We aren't pressing on without it."

She stared up at Jacques angrily, silently informing him this was not up for debate or something he could order her not to do. His jaw clenched and she could see his hands ball into fists at what was very clearly Pirogoeth asserting authority.

"We don't have to kill the dragon," she said in attempt to ease his concerns. "Merely distract it enough for someone to grab it. It won't be particularly interested in chasing us... we wouldn't represent a meal worth the effort."

Jacques was unconvinced. "Have *you* ever come across a snack you weren't interested in munching on?"

The mage decided that was a joke, and offered a bemused smile. "Come on. We're going to have to think of something to get that dragon to move."

So they returned to the team, and Alyth immediately asked, "So, how are we getting out of here?"

"We're not," Jacques answered, "Not yet. The mage wants us to fight a dragon."

"No..." Pirogoeth corrected before anyone could vocalize their protest. "*I'm* going to fight a dragon. *You* are going to recover my tome that it's sleeping on. It doesn't matter who gets it. Once one of you gets it, get back under cover. I'll let it chase me for a bit, then eventually it'll get bored once it realizes I'm no real threat."

"How can you be sure of that?" Goat asked.

"Dragons aren't mindless animals. It's believed they are of near or equal to human intelligence. They can also sense arcane energy. My scrying was probably what got its attention in the first place. I make myself a nice big target, and the rest of you won't even be worth the attention you give ants."

"Ants still get stepped on when we don't pay attention," Wiglaf countered.

The mage snapped, "Well, I'd hope all of *you* would be smart enough to not walk under a dragon's foot." She took a deep breath to calm herself. She wouldn't get their support by being insulting. "I know this sounds crazy. But we *need* that tome, and I need all of your help to do it."

Tyronica mustered her support first. "You can count on me."

Goat and Alyth looked at each other, then she said, "Us too."

Taylor stood to emphasize his agreement. "I'd follow you to the black hells."

Aurora clapped happily, "As would I!"

Wiglaf looked down, shrugged, and said, "I've always wanted the most dangerous hunts. What other Dayne could say they fought a dragon?"

Finally Jacques huffed, and said, "Alright. Then that's what we'll do. Just tell us where you wants us, Pirogoeth."

"The tunnel that Jacques and I scouted out the dragon, you all just wait there. I'll move in from the south. It should be obvious when that thing moves. Even if you somehow can't see it... you'll hear it."

Pirogoeth took off down the curving hall, soon all to herself as the rest of the team stopped at their designated point. She was torn with determination to reclaim her tome, and how the reasons she gave for doing so was a bit of a half-truth. While she had no idea just how useful it would be against the Winter Walkers, she *did* know it was vital for her research once she made it to Kuith. None of this mattered if she was useless in researching the Void when these adventures were done.

But she didn't dare tell them that. They wouldn't understand.

She chose the south side of the stadium because the dragon was laying in that direction, so that there would be little doubt that it would see her approach. Then to make sure it had her attention, she started channeling a fireball, assuming the rise in arcane energy would be worthy of notice.

And it was... at least enough for the dragon to open its eyes, the slitted pupils focusing directly on her. But it didn't regard her as enough of a threat to do more than huff a plume of smoke in the mage's general direction. She had been expecting that while hoping for a stronger response. It meant she had to become more of a nuisance, and that was concerning because she suspected an angry dragon would be considerably more dangerous than an annoyed one.

So Pirogoeth stepped forward aggressively and threw the fireball she cast. It did little other than crash against the dragon's stony scales, and caused the impact point to glow a dull orange.

The dragon responded by belching a plume of fire into the tunnel, and it was only that it lacked the focus of Pirogoeth's fireball that saved her life. She was able to react quickly enough to dive into the adjoining hall and magically shield herself from the flickers of flame that billowed after her.

Rock dragons *weren't* supposed to be fire-breathers, and that would make for a fabulous amendment to the *Arcana Historia* if she lived long enough to share it. When it didn't seem that any further attacks were coming, Pirogoeth stuck her head around the corner of the tunnel.

The dragon was back at rest, head down and its eyes closed. It's complete indifference would be comical if it hadn't been so insulting. Pirogoeth knew she was hardly any lethal threat to a dragon, but she should at least be worth more concern than *this*.

Pirogoeth charged into the courtyard, conjuring a fire storm right on the dragon's head. That got the wyrm to rear up at least, pushing it itself up by its front legs and roaring, the fire burbling within its throat creating a heat haze in the surrounding air.

Her charge into the courtyard was a dangerous gamble, but she had been correct. The dragon was hellbent on staying right where it was. A thought crossed her mind, and one that represented a far more dangerous gamble... but perhaps it was worth taking her chances.

Did the dragon *not* want to fight?

Testing the theory, Pirogoeth dropped her arms and stopped all channeling. She then held out her hands to display a lack of aggression before slowly stepping forward. Dragons *were* remarkably intelligent, after all... perhaps it would let her retrieve her tome and they could all leave in peace.

For those first few slow steps, it seemed like the dragon was going to be receptive to that idea. Then Jacques came out of the corner of her eye, tackling her aside. This was a life-saving move, because before Pirogoeth was taken down, the dragon's jaws snapped closed right where the mage would have been.

"Are you *insane*, woman?" the former pirate screamed as he scrambled to his feet, yanking on Pirogoeth's left arm sharply to pull her up while he had already broken into a run.

"I thought maybe the dragon wouldn't attack me!" Pirogoeth cried out defensively. "It wasn't moving after me!"

"Yeah, we noticed," Jacques grumbled sarcastically. "So what's the plan now?"

"I'm still thinking about that."

Alyth and Goat tried to apply cover with their bows, but shooting a rock dragon with arrows was rather like trying to pierce a brick wall with a piece of straw. Pirogoeth suspected the only reason their target reacted at all was because the two archers were yelling. It swung its tail in their direction, merely clipping the edge of the tunnel and causing it to partially collapse, with the gust generated by that swipe knocking Goat and Alyth flat on their backs.

Wiglaf charged into the fray, using the dragon's fragmented attention to drop his club onto its right rear paw, audibly cracking its toe and claw. This was actually a feat worthy of song, as doing *any* notable injury to a dragon required a tremendous amount of strength.

However, such songs had a tendency to end with the death of the hero, because breaking a dragon's toe doesn't exactly stop it from stomping you flat, gobbling you whole, or burning you to ash. And that would have been Wiglaf's fate if Pirogoeth hadn't made herself a greater annoyance with a fireball to the eye.

And through all that chaos, Aurora had managed to secure the black tome, winding around the dragons legs tentatively, creeping under its belly, and literally snatching the tome from between the dragon's toes. The great wyrm *immediately* turned it's attention to the healer that was making a break for the tunnel.

The tome itself was what the dragon was interested in, no doubt because of the energy it was *still* radiating despite not being channeled. It wasn't even swayed by another one of Pirogoeth's fireballs aimed at its face, instead ducking under the spell with surprising nimbleness for its size while taking a bite that would have easily gobbled up Aurora all at once if Tyronica hadn't tackled the healer to the ground.

Pirogoeth's fireball meanwhile had kept arcing upward, by chance striking one of the stadium lights. With a great shower of sparks, it overloaded then went dark, casting shadows onto the courtyard.

That was something the dragon noticed, and it shrieked, recoiling from the darkness. Seeing an opportunity and forcing herself not to think about the why at the moment, Pirogoeth called out, "Alyth! If you think you can hit the lights, do it!"

Pirogoeth took out two more lights along the east side that allowed an avenue for the team to escape, with Alyth targeting the south side to force the dragon back from pursuit. And while it certainly cowered away, it was not at all keen with allowing the party to escape. It led to another astounding discovery about dragons that Pirogoeth realized would potentially rewrite the entire book about them.

They could cast magic of their own.

It reared back on its haunches, lifted its head to the ceiling, and roared. Pirogoeth could *feel* the surge of arcane energy, then the entire stadium shook violently as the team retreated into the tunnel. "We need to keep moving!" Pirogoeth yelled. "This building isn't going to hold up against that!"

Pirogoeth was right. The team wound through the halls of the outer ring, and out what was no doubt a service entry, just as the north side of the stadium started to collapse. Where Pirogoeth was *wrong*, however, was the assumption that the cavern floor was going to hold.

It didn't.

The stone beneath them fell away abruptly, followed by their screams as they dropped into the unknown depths of the world...

Chapter Four: Pitch Black

Personally, Pirogoeth thought it was a minor miracle that she reacted in a way that saved their lives while she herself was tumbling to a certain demise. In truth, it was a stroke of luck that she guessed which way was up correctly, otherwise the gust of wind that slowed their meeting with the earth would have instead hastened it.

They touched down in a matter that wasn't exactly comfortable, but at least wasn't fatal or even significantly injurious. Pirogoeth immediately conjured her lighting cantrip to illuminate their surroundings and allow the team to take stock of the situation and each other.

Aurora took to healing what minor bumps and bruises the team had received while the rest tried to figure out exactly where they were. Whatever cavern they were in was so large that even the light wasn't reaching any wall, creating the feeling of a featureless stone island on a sea of darkness, where stepping out of the light meant you dropped off into nothing.

"I don't like this place..." Aurora whimpered, hugging herself as if she was cold.

Pirogoeth seconded that notion. There was something very wrong about being here, a chill that was more than magical or physical. The entire space itself felt wrong. "We shouldn't be here..." the mage said.

"Well, whose fault is that?" Wiglaf huffed grumpily.

"Don't even start," Jacques interrupted. "Plans go sideways. We've been over this. Any idea where we should go?"

Aurora shook her head, "I can't... feel anything other than dread."

"North for now," Pirogoeth decided, if only for the reason that Vazmeade was ostensibly somewhere in that direction. "I got a glimpse of the flow of the empire's magic. Not enough for a precise map, but a rough guess. I have no idea how accurate it'll be from this level, but it's a start."

The former pirate agreed, mostly because he had no better plan. "Tyronica, take point. Wiglaf, watch our flanks. Everyone else, stay close."

It could have taken an hour, or ten, slowly marching forward. Or maybe they were running. Or maybe they weren't moving at all. It was so hard to tell just how fast they were going or for how long when the surroundings never changed. Were they even in a cavern at this point? Or simply in a place the Coders forgot to make?

The latter thought was absurdly silly, of course, but it was a thought that really began to hook into her brain as the chill and dread got so intense that even the non-magically inclined members of the party started to feel it. Jacques voiced that opinion when abruptly ordered, "Stop! Nobody move!"

The entire team froze dead in their tracks. "What is the matter, sir?" Alyth asked.

"Just follow me and stay close."

"What is going on?" Tyronica asked with a voice that she no doubt meant to sound demanding, but instead was laced with uncertainty.

"I'll tell you when I confirm it. Now, come on."

She fell in step behind the former pirate, and he whispered quietly so that only she could hear, "I thought I saw something... rippling... just on the edge of the light, and a lot of things fell into place."

"Like what?" Pirogoeth asked.

"I've seen something like this before. I want to make sure, but I think I know what we're going to find."

Soon, Pirogoeth could see it too, a distinct ripple, like water... but unnervingly different. Even as they got closer, it didn't seem to cast any additional illumination on what they were seeing except that the light was slowly turning into a pale violet.

"Damn it all..." Jacques mumbled. "I knew it. That's dire water."

Pirogoeth didn't need an explanation, for it all fell into place herself. While she had never seen dire water before, she had read and been taught all about it religiously by her master, and reinforced by the few discussions she had with his contemporaries.

The Void was here. In the depths of the earth.

"We're turning west," Jacques informed.

"Agreed."

She was lost in thought as they made their return to the party. The Void... was already here. It didn't matter if it kept chewing up islands to the south, it would eat everything up from below *long* before then. The world had far less time than anyone had thought. Which made getting this damn war over sooner rather than later more important than ever before.

Even when Jacques informed the team of what they had found

as well as their new direction, Pirogoeth apparently looked perturbed enough for others to take notice. "What's wrong, P?" Aurora asked.

She shook her head to try and defuse concern. "I'm just thinking too far ahead again. We've got enough problems right in front of us for me to worrying about what comes next."

"If you need to talk about *anything*, you know I'm here."

"Thank you for that. And if I have anything worth sharing, I'll do so."

The healer hummed curiously. "Are you sure?"

"Yes..." the mage replied warily.

She smiled, "I'm sorry. I don't mean to sound so accusing. It's just... I've seen this particular tome before. Where did you get it?"

Pirogoeth blinked as Aurora handed over the black book, the mage having forgotten that Aurora had taken it during the fight with the rock dragon. Pirogoeth took it back with almost limp hands, focused on the red eye as if it was looking back at her. "You've... seen *this* one before?"

Aurora nodded. "Yes. Which is why I wondered where you got it."

Pirogoeth shrugged. "From my master. *He* got it through dubious means from a collector, as I understand. Where said collector got it... I couldn't say. Where did you see it before?"

"On a man who would meet my mother on occasion. I guess people like him would gather, and my mother rarely if ever went to those meetings. So he came to keep her up to date, give her things pertinent to her "duties", whatever those were... I never even knew his name. I don't even think I was ever supposed to know much about him because my mother would send me away whenever he arrived. But I do quite clearly remember that he carried this tome with the red eye."

Pirogoeth remembered the odd woman who Jacques claimed was an Administrator of the Gold Pirates. "Do you think your mother was a Gold Pirate?"

She shook her head. "If she was, she did nothing that it entailed, either in the traditional sense or how Sergeant Jacques described them."

Pirogoeth made a thoughtful sound. Maybe the two groups weren't inherently connected, and more of two separate organizations that shared similar goals, or something like all Gold Pirates Administrators were of the group, but not everyone of that group was a Gold Pirate administrator.

"Oh sweet mercy of the Coders!" Tyronica exhaled in relief.

Pirogoeth and Aurora snapped out of their discussion to discover why. The team had mercifully found the wall of this cavern and a roughly carved stone stairwell that went up. The team didn't need any orders, the only thing that they needed to do was determine an order because it was only wide enough for one person to climb at a time.

Nor did it go up very far... not nearly enough to get them back to the level they had been on. But they at least emerged onto what looked to be ground that had seen the touch of mortal hands.

This cavern was much narrower, with flakes of copper and iron veins dotting the rock and a rail running straight down the middle of it suggesting it was a mine shaft. They followed that shaft northwest until it broadened into what looked to be a hub to gather the mined metals and send them up to the surface. It certainly didn't seem anything like the carefully crafted and shaped stone of the empire of Quan'Dor.

"Hey, look at this!" Goat yipped, pointing to a steel panel fused to the wall, faded with time and age.

"This... isn't elven handiwork." Pirogoeth noted. "This is an ancient human language!"

"Really?"

"Yes!" the mage exclaimed. "This is Galean! They were one of the first northern empires, before they collapsed. It's believed that the survivors became the Daynes of our day!"

Wiglaf frowned, but acknowledged, "My people don't remember much of our past, but it is said before we became nomadic that we dug deep into the land. You likely know more than I do."

"And the significance of this is...?" Jacques asked, his voice trailing off to compel Pirogoeth to get to the point.

"The Galeans had fairly limited territory and didn't expand terribly far south. We're well within the Daynelands, and are *definitely* on the right track. It also means that there could be any number of tunnels that lead out of here!"

Goat pointed back at the marker, and asked, "Out of curiosity, what *does* this say?"

Pirogoeth shook her head. "Not much is legible, I'm afraid. The first line says 'Fr...something... bazz... and probably 'Mining Company' guessing from the context of what survived. The second line has the number six-hundred and eighty-eight which could be the year of this mine's opening, but since the Gales didn't use our calendar, that really doesn't tell us much. Anything below that has been weathered beyond any hope of reading. Now let's move. I'd rather get out of this mine before we all collapse from exhaustion."

She didn't air the *real* reason for her haste, because she was just putting together the clues herself and didn't want to panic the team with what she couldn't explain conclusively. But between the spidulls and the rock dragon, she had seen one consistent, and troubling, behavior.

All of those very deadly monsters of the underground were *terrified* of the dark, and there *had* to be a reason for that.

They picked the tunnel from the several that branched off from the hub due to many reasons. It was the only one that seemed to go up, it went northward, and it was the closest. And it did indeed seem like they had the right idea. But Wiglaf quickly observed an ill omen as they wound upward through the earth.

"I'm not smelling fresh air," the wolf shaman said. "I fear this is a dead end."

Pirogoeth knew he was right, but also knew that they weren't going to have time to wind back and choose another tunnel before exhaustion would become too strong to ignore. Their best chance was to see this through to the end and hope.

That hope was dashed harshly, especially when they discovered they hadn't been the only ones to find the end of this particular road.

The tunnel had been sealed, rocks dirt and rubble completely barring further passage either going in or coming out of the mine, confirming Pirogoeth's fears that there was something terrible down in the depths that the elves didn't dare let loose.

The party reached a different conclusion. "The elves *really* didn't want anyone getting into their underground empire, did they?"

Pirogoeth knew better. This wasn't the smooth, polishing shaping of Quan'Dor. This was a hastened demolition by someone, most likely the Galeans, discovering there was something in the depths beyond their power. Further confirmation of that theory came when she spied the remains of someone who had been in the mines earlier.

There wasn't much left, a rusted out lantern, the shredded remains of a pack, and a brown, leather bound journal.

"Am I the only one a little unnerved that there's no bones or anything else to signify who left this stuff here?" Goat asked.

Pirogoeth had picked up the journal, and asked Alyth, "Can you see if there's anything salvageable with that lantern?"

Alyth gave it a look over and shook her head, "Not even a

drop of oil we could use."

The mage expected as much, but it had been a fleeting hope. But even if Alyth hadn't given her assessment, Pirogoeth would have discovered the truth soon enough.

The journal had belonged to one of the handful of adventurers that braved the Great Underground Empire, a scholar from the Avalon city of River Bleu by the name of Tully, entering from the same open door that she and her party had used. He mentioned the same pristine ruins, asked the same questions she did.

Half of his team had been lost in initial skirmishes with the spidulls, not having her team's luck of entering Quan'Dor during the "night", though Tully had quickly figured out their quirky behavior, and then to proceed in the lower light while the chimeric beasts hid.

He also discovered why the spidulls feared the dark... though not exactly what was causing it.

Tully's team didn't take the same path Pirogoeth's did, their path going eastward where the Galeans had seemed to had dug into the Great Underground Empire long before. It was here that they encountered the monsters in the dark.

Pirogoeth read the relevant passage to the rest of the team. There was no longer any point trying to hide her suspicions. "Darcy lingered too far behind," She recited. "By the time we heard his screams and turned back, half of him was gone, torn asunder by a monster that I can only describe as shadow, teeth, and claws. It recoiled from the light, giving us the means to give what was left of our friend a proper burial, but now we understand the peril.

"The tunnels are sealed. The Galeans must have realized what they had released when they pierced the elven empire two thousand years ago. Hope is fading like the last flickers of light in this final lantern. It is nearly pitch black, and I am likely to be eaten by a gr..."

"By a what?" Alyth asked when Pirogoeth abruptly stopped.

Pirogoeth shook her head. "I don't know what he was going to call it. The lantern probably died mid-word."

"Maybe he was gurgling while being attacked?" Goat offered.

Alyth gaped at him in disbelief. "He wouldn't have *written it down* if that was the case!"

"Maybe he was dictating?"

The marksman quickly reached her limit. "Oh... *shut... up!*"

Her rage quickly dispelled however, and she took surprising initiative with a public display of affection, throwing her arms around his neck and burying her face in his shoulder. "I'm sorry... I... I know you're trying to lighten the mood."

He responded with a comforting hug. "It's okay. This is a pretty stressful situation."

Jacques inhaled deeply, and asked, "How much longer can you keep this light up, Pirogoeth?"

"Not long enough to explore every damn tunnel in this mine," the mage replied. "I suppose we can try to find the access point the previous party did, but I can't imagine that will be before I pass out from sheer exhaustion."

"Then that's what we're going to do people," the former pirate ordered, "And while we're looking, keep an eye out for *anything* that we could use to start a fire with. I have a hard time believing whoever these poor sots were got this far without *something* we can use."

That something might as well have been a needle in a haystack as the team backtracked to the mine hub again. If it wasn't metal, it didn't survive the years or whatever the hell was down here in the darkness. In desperation, Pirogoeth allowed them to sacrifice the journal's pages, but said pages were so dry and weathered by age that they flashed away far too quickly to form even a meager flame.

Pirogoeth *knew* how important it was to stay awake. Sleep was death, not just for her, but everyone with her. Yet there came a point where her body simply couldn't keep going.

It hadn't seemed like much to the rest of the party. Merely a stumble. But it was where the mage's vision blurred... and her cantrip blinked out.

Goat's scream was immediate. A rush of adrenaline followed by instinct saved him, a flare of pure light that scattered every single shadow beast that had been stalking them. The one that had snared Goat by the leg, had been caught, and the party got a good look at what they were facing before it vaporized into a puff of acrid smoke.

It had been humanoid... at least mostly. Where hands should have been were curved talons a foot long, if not more. It's head was misshapen to the point where it was half mouth, filled with a maw of fangs that curled down the monster's throat as it gaped in a silent scream.

But what Pirogoeth had noticed more was the elongated, pointed ears, that stuck out behind the miserable creature's twisted head.

Goat screamed again, clutching his leg, scored to the bone in several places in that mere blink of the light. While Pirogoeth dimmed her spell to what illuminated the party for no reason but to save her energy, Aurora rushed to work her own magic on the badly wounded scout.

"Mikael! Shh! You're going to be alright!" Alyth insisted, holding his head in her lap and stroking his hair. "Just keep still."

"You should be leaving me, keep going... while Pirogoeth is still awake."

"That wouldn't be nearly long enough for us to find an escape route," the mage replied glumly. "I'll... ignite a firestorm... maybe... it'll catch something flammable..."

Instead, a voice from the dark, like a song from a deeply scratched instrument, offered an alternative.

"That won't be necessary. Perhaps... you are the ones we've been hoping for. Ones that can finally rid us of the light."

Pirogoeth silently thanked Jacques for speaking, because the mage wasn't sure she could do so clearly. "What light? And why would we want to get rid of it for you?"

"Deeper in the mountain, where our traitor master betrayed us to this curse, where he continues to experiment with the Heart of the Empire. He lied to us, turned us into his immortal protectors, immune to our revenge while he bathes in the light of the Heart."

"You... you're the survivors of Quan'Dor, aren't you?" Pirogoeth asked.

"*Do not speak of that name again, arcanist!*" the voice bellowed. "Unless you want us to treat you as the elven people would."

"How about you start from the beginning, if you could?" Jacques interrupted. "Presuming we agree to help you, we'd like to know what exactly we're dealing with."

"I doubt I could stay awake that long," Pirogoeth admitted. "Black hells, I don't think I could stay awake another fifteen minutes."

"We will allow you to rest and sleep before escorting you to the master's hall," the voice promised.

"And we should believe ravenous monsters that could consume us in seconds?" Wiglaf asked.

"If eating us was their goal, they'd only have to wait," Pirogoeth grumbled in reminder.

From the darkness above, a bundle wrapped in a blood-stained tattered cloth and bound with suspect twine dropped in the center of the party. Opening it revealed kindling and wood for what could serve as a decent campfire.

"There. The light will keep us at bay if you do not trust us curbing our thirst for violence," the voice snarled. "We will return when you have rested."

The shadow monsters supposedly retreated, not that Pirogoeth was terribly inclined on trying another flare to prove that. Instead, she suggested, "Why don't one of you get that fired started while you can still see what you're doing? I'm about ready to pass out here."

Jacques nodded, "Hells, *all* of us are near dead on our feet, and *we* haven't been maintaining a spell all damn day. I don't even know how you went this long. Tyronica, help me out with this so that the poor girl can get some rest."

Pirogoeth knew she *had* to be exhausted, because she knew she *should* have a hundred questions running through her mind concerning what had transpired, but right at that moment, the only thing she cared about was getting this campfire started and her sleeping bag rolled out then slipping into blissful unconsciousness.

The mage extinguished her light cantrip the instant the tinder caught a solid flame that could ignite the thicker fuel logs. Taylor had taken the initiative to roll out her sleeping bag for her with the instructions, "Rest, little mage. You've earned it. For once, we'll watch out for you."

She wasn't sure where *that* sentiment came from, but by the time she had pulled the sleeping bag around her, her body forced her brain to cease any and all activity.

~   ~   ~   ~   ~

Pirogoeth jerked to alertness, quickly sitting up while her eyes focused and her mind desperately tried to grasp everything that been said, to partial success. As her vision clarified, she saw the rest of the team circled around the dying fire, their eyes turned to her warily. They had been engaged in an increasingly heated discussion, the volume of which had woken her.

"What... is going on?" the mage asked.

Jacques replied, "Nothing, really. Just some petty disagreements that have nothing to do with anything, but is better to talk about than whatever those things are that are going to escort us to dispatch whatever is waiting for us."

Pirogoeth highly doubted the first part, but knew the second part was true enough that it wasn't worth pressing the issue. "I take it you were all waiting for me to wake up?"

"Yes, arcanist," the voice from the shadows declared. "As you are essential to any hopes of overcoming the master of the mountain, it was essential you be well rested. Eat, then we will escort you to the light."

Jacques offered her a handful of jerky and some water in what looked like a wine skin. "Our hosts offered this stuff to us. It's probably best if you don't ask where it came from."

Pirogoeth certainly wasn't going to turn down food that wasn't from their supplies. One meal not taken from there was one meal longer they could go on their journey. But as she bit down and started chewing, the freshness and flavor simply made her ask.

"How did you make this?" she asked the shadows, "This had to have been prepared recently."

There was the sounds of muttering, before the voice replied, "While we are not entirely what we once were, we still have some of our ancestral magics."

While she *could* conjure fairly simple foodstuffs like bread and water, more complex items (like jerky) were rarely worth the energy needed to make of them. "That must have been difficult," she noted as she took her first bite. It was remarkably tender, with a hint of flavor that she couldn't quite put her finger on, like a mellow pepper, but with sweet tones that she had never experienced before.

"Our magic isn't like yours. Arcane power is not as efficient. Though... admittedly, it is more powerful and more adaptable. Ours is reliant on what is at hand. Yours creates from nothing."

Despite Jacques warning, Pirogoeth had to know. "Then what did you have on hand to make this?"

There was a *very* long and awkward silence before the answer. "Ourselves."

Jacques closed his eyes and heaved a deep sigh as Pirogoeth winced. "I told you that you didn't want to know," the former pirate mumbled. "And for the love of the Coders, if you value keeping your breakfast down, you *won't* ask how they learned our language."

She finished eating the jerky anyway, washing it down with the water. Perhaps it said something about life in the militia that she wasn't going to let that disclosure stop her from finishing a free meal. After giving the rest of her team the once over, she declared, "I think we're ready. Take us to this master of yours, and we'll see what we can do about the light that torments you."

Pirogoeth ignited her light as Jacques and Taylor extinguished the campfire embers, and the voice from the shadows ordered, "Start to the west. We will mark the stone in the direction you need to go."

The markings probably weren't needed, as their guide was remarkably chatty on the path to the point where it was pretty easy just to follow by the voice. "We were once elves of the empire of Quan'Dor, just as our master was, the Grand Shaper Azegbom."

"That's a mouthful of a name," Goat quipped.

"He was... peculiar in more than just his name. He was a master of chimerism, responsible for many of the creatures we bred to help us defend the empire as we lost ground to the more numerous humans and their arcanists. Even when we went underground and sealed ourselves, the fear was that one day the humans would find a way through our locks and invade."

"Not an undue concern," Pirogoeth admitted. "Considering we have an example of one human empire digging into Quan'Dor and your doors having been forced open. That's how we got here."

"The mithril doors were supposed to last a thousand thousand years. In truth, the human arcanists were gaining such power so quickly that they overpowered the magic holding the doors shut within decades. Our great shapers then tried to bury the doors behind the thickest hardest rock, but human miners were of incredible persistence. Quan'Dor was no refuge for my people, it was our tomb."

This was a part of history no one in the present knew. The belief was that once the elves sealed themselves away that the humans had stopped their pursuit. "So our ancestors continued to attack even after the elven retreat underground?" Pirogoeth asked.

"Yes. And as I said before, it was not even two of your generations that they had penetrated into our sanctuary. We held for a little while, though your kind probably considers a century a long time, but the invasion came from every direction, none of our doors held, and none of our shaping held your people back."

"Why were we so persistent in exterminating you?"

"Because we refused to follow the Coders will. We were *intended* by the Coders to cede control of the world to humans once it was deemed ready. But we refused. We sought to subjugate humanity, keeping them under our heel by executing any human children that showed signs of the arcane power that was meant to supplant our shaping. But our efforts were in vain. Humans bred faster than we could control, thrived in places we could not easily reach, and were blessed with the tomes that allowed them to more effectively harness their greater power. The memory of our crimes passed down over generations, and blessed by the Coders to make us pay."

Wiglaf hummed, and said, "These Coders seem much more

vengeful than modern man describes them. Perhaps they deserve more credit than I have given them."

Pirogoeth rolled her eyes. Of course Wiglaf would respect the Coders if they were barbaric genocidal monsters.

The voice continued, "In our darkest hour, Grand Shaper Azegbom offered what he claimed was salvation. Firstly, he released the driders; chimeric beasts of spider and bull. You no doubt had seen them in the upper empire. Fast breeding like the humans, sensitive to magic, and certifiably deadly. But he had made the monsters in haste, they did not discern elf from human, did not make any distinction between shaping and arcane. They killed elf as easily as human, hastening our demise. For a long time, I thought it to be an accident... but perhaps it was by design."

"*Driders*." Goat repeated, then turned to Alyth and added, "I actually like that a lot better than 'spidull' or 'bullder' honestly."

Pirogoeth ignored the scout's quip, and asked, "Design? You think the Grand Shaper *intended* to kill everyone?"

"I am not *certain*, but it's possible considering his second action. As we were forced out of our capital, our numbers dwindling, Azegbom came to us again, offering us a chance at survival, though not a blessed one. In our desperation to avoid being slaughtered by monsters and humans alike, those of us that dwell down in these depths agreed. We were fused with the shadow itself, turning us into what you now experience, unable to suffer even the slightest light, cursed to prowl the darkness for eternity and unable to confront the Grand Shaper in the glow of the Heart of the Empire."

"And that's where we come in," Jacques noted.

"Your arcanist is the most powerful explorer any of us have ever encountered. She could challenge and defeat Azegbom, and take the light away. We will even show you a path back to the upper levels, where any number of doors would lie open for you to leave this dead land. At this point, all we desire is to languish in the dark without any further reminders of what we are and where we came from."

Pirogoeth agreed, "I... we'll do all we can."

"We will remember this."

"And we'll remember you not eating us!" Goat interjected.

Another awkward silence was followed with, "To be honest, human meat is stringy and not very tender. It's doubtful you would have been any tastier than the others that met their doom here."

It was something, Pirogoeth figured.

"We are coming up on the master's domain. I ask that you

extinguish your light, arcanist, so that I and my brethren can pass through. You'll be able to see the glow of our master and his work around the next bend. Good luck, and may it pass unneeded."

Pirogoeth complied by extinguishing her cantrip and did indeed see a pale white glow reflecting off a bend in the increasingly smooth rock of the tunnel.

"So, right around this corner is an ancient wizard from a time long before history. All we have to do is kill this no doubt nigh-godly power and take whatever is lighting his home," Alyth commented sarcastically. "How hard could that possibly be?"

Pirogoeth looked back towards the darkness, and the miserable souls condemned to a lightless hell simply because they didn't want to die. She then took the lead towards the light that was honestly secondary in her mind behind the fact that Grand Shaper Azegbom had a *lot* to answer for...

Chapter Five: The Wizard of Quan'Dor

The turn led to a wide rectangular room of a shimmering metal that must have been done by the hands of an experienced shaper. The angles of the corners were sharp, the walls level and smooth, and without the slightest use of brick or mortar, with shelves molded right out of the walls to each side.

The shelves themselves were empty and clearly had not been used for a while, as Goat displayed a thick layer of dust as he drew his finger across the nearest surface.

Pirogoeth was also touching the walls, though not to reflect on their disuse. "This is... incredible. If Azegbom did this, he is such an experienced shaper that he could separate metal from rock before working with it."

"Getting second thoughts on your ability to defeat this man?" Jacques asked.

"I didn't have *first* thoughts to begin with," the mage admitted. "But we're looking at a degree of magical aptitude I can't even fully comprehend, much less plan against."

"Well, if this is any indication, maybe the guy is dead already?" Tyronica suggested.

"That would be tremendously fortunate," Wiglaf groused. "Tell me how many times that has happened for us again?"

Tyronica's theory, however, seemed to bear some weight as they crossed the room into a main hall and took the first right into a circular, domed laboratory. Tables raised and fused to the floor joined the shelves, these topped with flasks and containers that were still full of concoctions and elixirs that had quite clearly suffered with age.

Alyth experimentally sniffed the top from a flask on a circular table in the center, then coughed violently as the aged vapors hit her. Pirogoeth immediately pushed her away saying, "Don't do that! Coders know what any of this stuff has decayed into! Aurora, detoxify her just to be safe!"

Pirogoeth began carefully assessing the contents of the room, because while she didn't know much (if anything) of how elves researched their magic, this setup was much more akin to how she knew *humans* of the earliest empires did *their* research into arcane energy.

"What are you looking for, Pirogoeth?" Jacques asked as the mage carefully started examining dry stock on a shelf along the far side of the perimeter.

"Nothing specifically," she replied as she took a pinch of what she identified as fire powder from a stone urn and let it run through her fingers. "Just intrigued. These are all apothecary materials, substances used in releasing arcane energy without the use of tomes. I'm curious why Azegbom was doing similar research. Why arcane energy, something that by all accounts the elves couldn't use, was something he was experimenting with."

"Here's hoping we never get the opportunity to find out," Jacques declared. "Let's move on and find this 'light' that our friends in the shadows were talking about."

It was fairly fascinating how the light within Azegbom's lair didn't seem to be coming from any one single source, though there didn't appear to be any multiple sources from where it could be coming from either. Even the next room didn't show any indication of the source, nor any signs of life.

They crossed the hall and entered what they had become accustomed to seeing in an elven bedroom; a silk hammock moored to three corners of the room, though far larger than what they had seen before with a low elongated wardrobe underneath, and a corner desk in the fourth one, though lacking a chair for sitting. None of the furnishings had shown any signs of being used in an incredibly long time, as when Tyronica erupted into a coughing fit just trying to open one of the wardrobe's shelves and getting a plume of dust in her face for the trouble.

Pirogoeth herself examined the desk for any clues, though she didn't expect to find much useful information. While he had literal reams of parchment stored in the cabinets below the desk surface, it was all in the ancient elven language that she couldn't hope to translate.

The desk surface featured a badly shredded piece of parchment and a remarkably complex ink pen with the ink reservoir *inside* the stem of the pen itself, a feature she was able to note because the pen had been crudely snapped in half.

Her eyes then turned to a shattered picture frame roughly six inches to a side that had fallen from its mount molded to the table, three of the pieces barely clinging to each other and forming what might have been a portrait of Azegbom himself, though it was hard to make out any details from remained of the faded colors and damaged canvas other than an elven man with dark hair.

"Pirogoeth?" Aurora asked, startling the mage.

She looked up to see the team waiting at the doorway or back in the main hall. "Sorry. I guess I get lost in the details easily," she apologized.

Once she squeezed back into the hall with the rest of the team, Jacques pointed directly ahead. "How about we skip the rest of the tour, and just go into the big room down that way?"

"Are ya sure?" Goat asked. "We haven't found the bathroom yet. His droppings could be illuminating."

Jacques's lips turned upwards in disgust. "Unless they're glowing, I doubt it, and if they are, I don't wanna know about it. Now move."

The room at the end of the hall was indeed larger. *Much* larger, in a dome much like the entry, but at least five times the size and strewn with piles of debris from shattered stone bookshelves, various trinkets, and piles of valuable metals like gold and silver all around the perimeter.

Goat quickly pointed out the composition of the walls and floors. "Look... the area right in front of us is made of the same metal as the rest of Azegbom's space, but the rest is molded out of straight stone. Stone that gets rougher and less refined the further out and further up you look."

"You think Azegbom was expanding on this place?" Alyth asked.

"And with increasingly less finesse too," Goat replied, "I wonder why. Whattya think, P?"

Not that Pirogoeth or Aurora were paying attention to anything else than the shimmering translucent white faceted jewel the size of a large coconut sitting on top of a dais from from spines of twirled gold. "I've... never seen a focusing crystal that big before." Pirogoeth stammered, awestruck.

"An untainted one, at that," Aurora mumbled. "Any focusing crystal I've ever encountered had already been blooded."

"Blooded?" Tyronica asked.

"You know how you'd see me use my own blood to assist in my scrying?" Pirogoeth explained, though she never took her eyes off the focusing crystal as she and Aurora reverently approached the gigantic artifact. "Mages would taint a focusing crystal with their blood for a similar reason, to more efficiently process the power it generated. It would inevitably turn a focusing crystal red rather than its natural color."

"It's doubtful blooding even *works*," Aurora added. "But it's become such a practice that you rarely, if ever, see an untarnished focusing crystal nowadays. This is... beautiful."

The two women were so ensorcelled by the sight that they didn't process the massive chamber shudder as if hit by a minor earthquake, or the clutter along the perimeter noticeably shift. That wasn't so much a problem, as the rest of the team made sure the pair was made quite well aware.

"Hey, P, is the room *supposed* to be moving like this?" Goat asked, catching Alyth as the marksman stumbled, then both of them falling hard to the floor when Wiglaf tripped backwards and crashed into them.

"And what in the black hells is *that*?" Jacques asked, his finger pointing towards the south side, and Pirogoeth catching a glimpse of something brown and scaled and very, very large slithering from underneath the rubble.

"Aurora... step back from the crystal..." Pirogoeth warned, her eyes widening as she followed her own advice. Aurora reluctantly obeyed, though whether or not it was necessary as the grotesque monster finally emerged from the periphery.

Pirogoeth found she was actually having a hard time parsing what exactly she was looking at. She was certainly used to chimeric monsters, but this was something beyond what she had experience in. It had the body of a snake... albeit an absurdly large snake even greater than the pythons that once lived in the jungles of Canno at least thirty times over. And while she had never seen a python, she had read and heard enough about them to know that they didn't have legs and paws like a bear like the one that dropped down to the right of the golden dais in the center of the room. Another fell behind and to the left, giving the monster the leverage it needed to hover over focusing crystal and the party as they formed a protective circle.

Alyth backed into Pirogoeth and nearly knocked her over, but for honestly good reason, as the monster's tail had pulled in her direction, a bulbous barbed tip like a scorpion drawing to within inches of the marksman's face. Perhaps astonishingly, that kept Pirogoeth's interest for but a fraction of a second because she found herself far more engrossed by the grotesque face that was assessing the party beneath it.

It was a face of many faces, really. A head topped with thin, scraggly silver hair framing a crown of horns with varying curves and lengths that Pirogoeth identified as the horns of a basilisk, a creature long thought extinct, much like the right eye, brow, and cheek that resembled a troll's. The remainder of the face was elven, if disfigured by the stinger of a wasp protruding from its chin.

It hadn't attacked any of the party yet, so it seemed safe for Pirogoeth to say, "I assume *you* are Grand Shaper Azegbom?"

Its eyes focused on the mage, and she could see both pupils, circular and slitted, narrow as it did so. Judging from the elven features, she sensed it was concentrating mightily on something until she felt a sting in the back of her head. She winced from the pain, but hurriedly waved off concern. She had heard of such techniques used by great wizards of the past, and suspected it was no attack.

She had been right. The creature exhaled sharply, betraying a moment of fatigue. "I have so little of my old magics that even something so meager drains me, but that was necessary," it finally replied with words she found she could understand in a deep voice that reflected its tremendous size. "At any rate, if you must use names for what I used to be, then yes. Though now, as I'm sure you can see, I am far more monster than elf."

Its face snaked downward to get a closer look at Pirogoeth, and it took all the courage she could muster to prevent recoiling. The thing smelled foul, like if a skunk had rolled about in carrion. "With what little of my senses remain, I could feel someone of considerable power approaching. I would not have expected by treasonous guards to have recruited such aid. What brings such a vibrant arcanist into the depths?"

Pirogoeth answered, "It's as you suspected. Your guards sent us here in the hopes of taking 'the light,' which I presume is referring to this focusing crystal between us."

Azegbom hummed thoughtfully, "Well, obviously, I can't have that. Even if I can't use it as it is intended, it's the only thing that keeps me from being torn apart by those grues out there."

"Grues?"

"Elven compound word of sorts, no doubt one that had no corollary in your tongue to be translated properly. 'Grun' meaning 'shadow,' and 'sues' meaning 'lesser ones.'"

Pirogoeth's eyebrows rose in curiosity. "Lesser ones?"

"Of course," Azegbom replied, "They were peons. Insignificant vassals of the dales that had wanted to throw their lives away to the driders after they had turned on us. They were fortunate I offered them an option to live at all. Treasoners. They *should* be grateful I deigned to give them a purpose."

Pirogoeth replied, "Well, we sadly can't go back without this crystal, or we'll be torn asunder by those grues."

Azegbom hummed again, "And thus we reach our impasse, haven't we? Because while I could certainly kill all of you easily enough, and don't pretend I couldn't. Even you, arcanist, would not be able to deal a fatal blow before I slaughtered all of you..."

"I'd be willing to take that bet," Wiglaf snarled as he gripped his club.

Pirogoeth shushed him, "*I* wouldn't take that bet."

"And that is why you are the wise one, and him the mindless slab of meat you hide behind to perform real acts of accomplishment," the twisted shaper mused. "Tragic how dumb oafs love to think they have any insight to offer, no? Seems that is as true for humans as it was elves."

Shamefully, Pirogoeth wasn't as much disgusted with what the shaper was saying as much as the fact he was saying so brazenly without any concern about how those "beneath him" would take it. Hearing some of her darkest thoughts being voiced put a weight on them that made Pirogoeth feel *very* uncomfortable with herself. It made her feel like a *worse* person, in a perverse way.

Wiglaf, as expected, didn't exactly take the dismissal with aplomb. "You abortion of..."

"You will be silent for once in your life, Dayne," Pirogoeth spat angrily, "Or I will let Azegbom stomp you flat!"

"Thank you, my dear arcanist," Azegbom said thankfully as Wiglaf looked about a second from attacking Pirogoeth instead. "Now, how to solve you little conundrum, hmm? Perhaps... could it be possible, I wonder?"

"Could *what* be possible?" Pirogoeth asked.

"Well, to teach you shaping magic, in a sense. As I've mentioned, there's little I can use the heart of the empire for, but you... might just be able to do it."

"Why me?" Pirogoeth asked, "Aurora here is of elven blood."

Azegbom turned his eyes in the healers direction and snorted. "Bah! No. Far too thin, her pool of energy far too narrow. You on the other hand, if through nothing but brute force, could no doubt shape a tunnel through the mountain with the help of this focusing crystal, I'd fathom."

"You think so?"

"Possibly. Human magic is normally so... inefficient, but they quickly discovered using these that they could harness more of the energy that was normally wasted. Between that and the tomes granted of our creators, as you might have guessed, even a handful of your arcanists overwhelmed even our strongest shaping. Such an indignity, by the by, that all our careful craftsmanship was thwarted with such ease with such sloppy spell casting. It's worth the attempt."

Jacques wondered, "If it was simply a matter of shaping a tunnel out of the mountain, why haven't you done it?"

Azegbom took a scornful glance at the pirate, but deigned not to answer until Pirogoeth admitted curiosity of that very question. "As you can surely see, I am at this point a chimera of so many different things I've spliced together just to sustain my life that I'm more animal than elfin. With it, came the unfortunate circumstance that the blood from which my shaping flows has become too thin myself to properly shape anything."

The shaper tilted his head upward. "Look at my lair, for example, look at how crude my last attempts to expand it was. By the time I realized my folly, it was far too late. My last attempt to fuse my being with another, a basilisk that I had initially hunted, proved to be the end of that."

"You needed to constantly merge yourself with other things, but the grues outside do not," Pirogoeth noted.

"And if I had the sense then that I do now, I would have probably done something similar. Fused with something inherently non-corporeal like the darkness had severely crippled their limited magic, but meant they could sustain themselves indefinitely. I, meanwhile, had thought I would have found an answer to my research long before my blood would thin beyond use."

"Yes, we saw your laboratory. You were experimenting with arcane energy, weren't you?"

Azegbom's lips curled upward in delight, "Oh brilliant you are, little human. Yes, that was *exactly* what I was doing! I had been so enraged at the fall of our empire, I thought surely if I could learn how to spellcraft the way the humans do, with my inherent advantages, that I alone could emerge into the world and crush the humans with ease! Oh... but that was not to be. The tomes of man do not speak to me, and the crystals that you use to focus your inherent gifts are nothing more than mere batteries to an elf. Such a waste of time. Such a waste."

"And yet you think *I* can be successful going the other way around?" Pirogoeth said skeptically.

"Yes, if for no reason than I discovered that arcane magic was more... versatile. No, you can't do the actual shaping magic of the elves. But you could feasibly do a suitable mimicry of it that would at least complete the task needed of you."

"And what would you get out of this? What would escaping now accomplish for you?"

Azegbom laughed so hard it shook the walls. "Hah! To exact my revenge on you filthy humans, of course! I may not be able to scour you all from the lands in this form, but imagine the damage I could do nonetheless!"

Pirogoeth could think of several reasons why that would be a bad idea, and only one of them had to do with Azegbom actually doing any serious damage on his own. Not that she doubted he could... but the idea of a monstrosity of titanic size, strength and ferocity, ensnared by the Winter Walkers was not a pleasant one. "That... might not be prudent, oh great shaper. See, there are..."

The grand shaper snarled with a reverberating sound that couldn't have come from any elven lungs. "If you do not, I'll kill all of you and eat all of you up here and now. How is *that* for prudence?"

"Not at all" was the thought going through Pirogoeth's mind, though she obviously didn't dare voice such. It was a minor miracle that the rest of her party understood the peril enough to keep their mouths mostly shut. She sincerely hoped that they were going to trust her on this... because this was going to take a lot of improvising and not a lot of back talk.

"I suppose we'll have to aid each other, then settle further matters once that bridge is crossed," the mage reluctantly declared. "And I will have access to this crystal then?"

Azegbom assured, "Obviously. You'll need a tremendous amount of energy, far more than an elf would, in order to safely dig through the rock of this mountain. After which, you can keep it for all it matters to me, and I'll spare you as we part ways. Do we have an agreement?"

Pirogoeth's mind had already started whirling as she acquiesced. "Yes, I suppose we do. But I must admit that I don't know any spell that could mimic what a shaper does."

Azegbom exhaled distressingly, "Of course not. Which is why you will need to *make* one."

Pirogoeth blanched at the very idea. Spell *creation* was a very dangerous path, one that Socrato had told her not to even *attempt* considering how his own explorations into alchemy had nearly killed him. In fact, Pirogoeth couldn't think of any mage in recorded history that had done so. Every spell that humans had in their arcane knowledge had been constructed and originally transcribed long before by hands assumed to have been the Coders'.

"Oh do not look so!" the shaper hissed, "Have you forgotten my own research? While I most certainly cannot use arcane might, I have most assuredly figured out the way of transcribing that energy into the tomes that you use. And besides, if you fail, then you die anyway. What do you have to lose?"

Pirogoeth muttered, "Well, when you put it that way..."

"Excellent!" Azegbom replied with the monster's equivalent of a happy chirp, "Now, go quickly now! In my lab there should be plenty of materials to inscribe a book with the spell we're going to be creating!"

Pirogoeth bowed respectfully, then gestured to the team to follow her back into the hall and towards the smaller domed room at the other end of Azegbom's lair. The minute Jacques thought they were out of earshot, she sided up to the mage and whispered, "Are we *seriously* working with that thing?"

"Yes," Pirogoeth answered crossly.

"That thing is *insane!* And you are going to help it *escape?*"

"Yes, it undoubtedly is. It's also not wrong. If *we* want to escape these depths, it's only going to happen with its favor."

The former pirate wasn't exactly going to be mollified by that. "And then what happens? We let it go do whatever the black hells it wants?"

Pirogoeth shook her head, "Hardly. I doubt it has any intention of letting us go after we're free of the underground empire. Confrontation is inevitable, it's merely a matter of where said confrontation takes place. I'd rather it be where there could feasibly be room to maneuver."

Pirogoeth silently tried to relay that she had a plan, not daring to air her thoughts as she didn't have *nearly* Jacques's confidence about being out of earshot. Instead, she took a slight detour into Azegbom's study, took some parchment and one of his pens, then began issuing orders while writing down her instructions.

"Now, this is what we will need, and I'm writing it down so you sots don't manage to forget. Wiglaf, vellum, at least three rolls. It's over there on the top east shelf. Goat, those narrow pans, see if there's any enchanted ink that hasn't dried out into sludge. If there is, we won't have to make more. Aurora, I think there's some leather binding on the southeast side. We might not need it if we're just making up one spell, but doesn't hurt to have some just in case."

Meanwhile, she was scribbling furiously and pointing to make sure the team was paying attention.

*I have an idea. Please don't ask
questions, you have to trust me.*

They seemed to trust her enough to follow her instructions at least. Goat gave her further hope for the success of her plan when he reported, "If what was in here was ink at some point, it isn't now."

This *was* good news, as the process of making enchanted ink for transcribing spells was not a quick process, and allowed her precious time to contemplate the details of her potentially suicidal scheme. She mused on such things while ordering Alyth on one of the vital tasks. "Alyth, do you see how some of these shelves have rusted?"

The marksman nodded, identifying the telltale red-orange tarnish quite easily. "Remarkable they aren't in worse shape considering how long they must have been standing."

"Can you... collect some of that rust for me?"

Now Alyth gave her a questioning side eye. "*Collect* it?"

"Yes. Scrape off as much rust as you can. I'll need it. Aurora, can you get the fire powder we saw earlier for me?"

The healer complied, as Alyth took to her task warily. "These are odd ingredients for ink."

"It's not for the ink, it's for the crystal. It'll come in handy when I start channeling through it. As for the ink, I'll need to find those myself. The sort of ink that I need is something that can only be made from particular ingredients, and the untrained eye likely won't be able to tell the difference."

In truth, the "trained" eye in this case was simply an affinity to magic. Enchanted ingredients were almost always kept in a dry state, as it gave them incredible longevity, apparently to the tune of thousands of years. A hint of magic kissed graphite, infused gummy sap, then reconstituted with a hint of simple mineral oil and mixed with a mortar and pestle.

She finished just in time for Alyth to return with a velvet pouch filled with rust shavings. "Excellent," she said, pointing to the tabletop next to a small ceramic urn of fire powder. "Put it right there and I'll get to it once I'm done mixing here. Wiglaf, Jacques... could you take the table behind me into the main chamber? I'm going to need it over there to actually pen the spell while Azegbom gives instruction."

With the ink ready, she filled a dusky colored inkwell, then took another mortar and pestle to grind down the rust flakes into a powder. This was actually a remarkably delicate measurement, as the ratio of powders was essential to get the reaction she wanted, and Azegbom's measuring tools were *not* in units she was familiar with. Too little of one or too much of the other, and it wouldn't generate the amount of heat she would need.

Her arm started to ache from the grinding, and after at least five minutes she stopped and examined all her work. She hoped it would be good enough on all counts. "Alright, let's go back to the main chamber, everyone..."

It was right at that moment that she saw it. The mage had no idea how she missed it, as it would have been next to her left hand as she had been grinding the ingredients for her ink. Perhaps she had unconsciously dismissed it as a regular piece of silver until she had moved and it reflected the light in a way that normal silver didn't.

It was a piece of mithril silver, the distinguishing features readily apparent now that she was actually looking for them. It had a much more evident shine and luster, and was heavier than normal silver. Socrato had kept pieces from his dabbling in alchemy, having considered it and blood lead to be the most promising candidates for his research.

She picked up the shard and spun it about in her hands. Maybe five inches long and two inches thick, shaped into a oblong oval. Compared to its more common mithril cousin, mithril silver was both heavier and softer, and as a result wasn't nearly as sought after except in jewelry. An even rarer form, like the sample she was holding was capable of holding and radiating magical energy that mages loved to use for alchemical experiments.

The mage found herself considering another option to deal with Azegbom, one that she had little doubt would be able to kill the chimeric monstrosity...

… And likely everyone else in the process.

She shook her head clear of the thought. No, that idea was patently insane.

"Pirogoeth?" Aurora asked, gently tapping her on the shoulder. "Is... something wrong?"

The mage shook her head, hastily shoving the shard into the reagents pouch on the side of her satchel. "Oh no, sorry. Everything's fine. Just got a little too lost in thought. I think we're as ready as we're going to be."

They weren't *exactly* ready, as Pirogoeth had to send Aurora back to Azegbom's study to retrieve an empty pen and funnel so that they could fill it with the enchanted ink she had made. With that delay, Pirogoeth decided to take the opportunity to apply her fire powder mixture to the focusing crystal.

"And... *what* are you doing with *that*, arcanist?" Azegbom queried with suspicion.

Apprenticing under a man who was as adept at sniffing out mistruth as Socrato had taught Pirogoeth one remarkably specific yet useful skill; how to lie with the truth. "This is a concoction that my people have found increases the amount of energy that mages can use in their tasks. We're not entirely certain *why* it works the way it does, and I might not even *need* it, but I'd rather have too much power to work with than not enough."

The chimeric shaper's eyes narrowed, but he clearly didn't sense any deceit as he pulled back away from the crystal's dais with a wary hum.

Aurora then returned with the items in question, and as Pirogoeth filled the pen she decided this was a design she would have to replicate. So much cleaner and long-lasting to have the ink stored inside the pen's reservoir and slowly seeping down through the tip rather than the quills and inkwells common above.

But with that minor snag resolved, it was time to get to the task of *creating* a spell which, despite all the dangers involved and the perils hovering over them, was something that Pirogoeth was finding herself tremendously excited about. Socrato certainly taught her much of the "how," but had not given her the opportunity to actually *do* it.

And for all its assured insanity and malicious intentions, Grand Shaper Azegbom certainly *did* know what he was doing.

"Now, let's begin with a focusing rune," it advised as Pirogoeth began forming the first lines onto vellum. "What you're looking for is a cone of energy, but shaped much like a corkscrew."

Pirogoeth nodded. "Ethereal magic; not my specialty, but more than doable." She added a spiral then a confinement rune to the spell to create the "shell" that the arcane energy would fill.

"Next, you'll want a rotation rune."

At that point, she was starting to get a hint of what Azegbom was looking for her to accomplish. "It's a drill! You're going to have me drill a tunnel up and out to the surface!"

"Brilliant!" Azegbom remarked. "I see you are familiar with the practice?"

She nodded, her genuine enthusiasm for the validity of the

concept hiding her glee that it would play nigh perfectly into her own schemes. "Indeed I am! This was one of my master's designs, well... similar, at least. Though he was designing it to be made with Reahtan steel rather than magic, so that a mage wouldn't have to be present for the mining."

Tyronica asked, "Socrato thought of this too? And that's *evidence* this will *work?*"

Pirogoeth eyed the Aramathean soldier crossly. "As eccentric as he is, I can't say I've seen plans of his that *haven't* worked to some degree. Yes, I dare say this entire plan has a chance... provided we actually form this spell correctly. Writing it down's the easy part, getting it to take is completely another."

Truth was, there didn't seem to be any rhyme or reason why some spells would copy and some would not. You could transcribe a spell perfectly to form from its previous iteration, and no magic would attach to the tome. Some could have significant flaws that weakened the spell or even it altered it in unpredictable ways and it would absorb magic without a problem. Pirogoeth couldn't imagine creating an entirely new spell would be any different.

She took a deep breath, held it, then released it slowly in a span of ten seconds. This was the part that Pirogoeth had never been allowed to do, merely study. Magic was a fickle thing when not bound into tomes or stored within an elven body. It didn't like being restricted, and the feedback when it was being compressed into a physical vessel could be extremely dangerous if not fatal. In addition, the mage had to move all this energy through nothing but their own force of will, as the process of channeling two separate things and maintaining them without even a moment's break in focus was simply beyond the human mind.

To the magically insensitive, it no doubt looked like Pirogoeth was doing nothing except sweating for no reason.

Wiglaf huffed, "Is she going to do something, or what?"

Azegbom hissed at the Dayne in a voice that was even louder than the initial interruption. "This is a *very* delicate process where concentration is paramount. Do still your wretched tongue before I still it *permanently.*"

Tyronica muttered, "You're being louder than he is..."

Aurora tapped her foot and shushed all three of them with an animated gesture towards the exit. "If you must talk, please take it outside."

Azegbom was about to note that wasn't really an option when

Pirogoeth grumbled, "It's moot, at this point. It's done." She wiped the sweat from her forehead, sighed, and said tiredly, "It worked. I... made my very own spell."

Aurora hugged her from behind, "Fantastic! I knew you could do it!"

Goat blinked rapidly, then pointed at the vellum. "That's it? No poofs or flashes of light?"

Pirogoeth shrugged and replied, "That's it. The show isn't in the making, but in the doing. But I'm afraid, Grand Shaper, that it will have to wait until I've rested some."

"Oh!" Azegbom replied, "Yes, of course, I can only imagine that was exhausting. Do feel free to use my chambers down the hall. Your entourage will need to scrounge up their own floor space, but I'm sure they're used to it."

Pirogoeth complied, the team following her as much to not be alone with Azegbom as any particular fatigue.

"So, whatcha gonna call it?" Goat asked Pirogoeth.

Her brows furrowed, she didn't have the energy to deal with this right now. "Call what?"

"Your spell! Don't all spells have interesting names?"

"It's not so much as a spell as it is a scroll," Pirogoeth corrected. "It's not even in a proper tome. It might damn near crumble into dust after the first time I cast it."

"So you're not going to name it?"

"No. I'm really not," the mage snapped. "Right now, I'm focused on getting a short break so I can dig us all out of here and into a whole different fire."

"A hole you dug us *into* to begin with," Wiglaf reminded.

Jacques shut that idea down in a hurry. "A hole we *all* dug, Dayne. You could have walked away from that silver door at the start of this just as much as anyone."

Tyronica grinned deviously and quoted, "The wolf doesn't fear the unknown, the unknown fears the wolf. Remember *that* little line?"

Goat jumped to her defense as well, "And it was *my* idea to come down here, if you remember, not P's. She's done a damn amazing job just to get us this far. So if you want someone to abuse, turn your venom on me."

Wiglaf clenched his jaw, and didn't speak further, and any rejoinder Pirogoeth was considering fell silent as well. The wolf shaman wasn't exactly wrong, but the other members' quick reprisals helped her morale as she drug herself through the doorway, then used a boost from Jacques to get up into the hammock.

"You're doing as well as you can, and a damn spot more than any of the rest of us," Jacques reassured.

"I'll get us out of this mess," Pirogoeth said confidently, "Granted... just to throw us into another fire, but that's how it goes in the adventuring life, right?"

He patted her on the shoulder, then slumped down to a sitting position on the near side of the door, Aurora already cross-legged at the far side.

"You don't have to get *too* comfortable," Pirogoeth said, hoping that her voice carried to the rest of the team that had spread out and across the hall. "I don't need to sleep or anything, just get a little breather and regain my energy."

From somewhere down the hall, she could hear Goat ask, "So no time for a quick tryst?" followed by the sound of Alyth, presumably, punching him.

"Hey, I want to get out of here as much as you do. I'm not going to waste your time."

Aurora agreed, "We can't forget that there's a big war on the surface, and they're counting on us to challenge and defeat the Winter Walkers as quickly as we can."

"But we *also* aren't going to let you push yourself until you're good and ready, got it?" Jacques warned. "I can't imagine digging through a mountain is going to be easy on you, rested or not."

Pirogoeth smiled ruefully and looked out into space, feeling the strength slowly return to her muscles. There was a part of her that *had* forgotten about the war above, and that subtle reminder was one she needed. It wasn't like she was going to feel any less pressure if she gave it a good night's sleep.

But it did allow herself a half hour of rest before the anticipation finally forced her to declare, "Alright, thanks for waiting. I'm as ready as I'm going to be."

Jacques was skeptical. "Are you sure?"

"Just needed to rebuild my energy, not sleep off fatigue," she insisted. "I'm good to go."

Jacques and Aurora helped her out of the hammock, and let her took the lead back to Azegbom's main chamber. The chimera's head perked up in anticipation as the team returned, and it said hopefully, "Are we ready to finally be free of this underground hell?"

Pirogoeth nodded, "We are indeed."

Azegbom then instructed. "Then I would suggest you begin

on the north side of this room, just to the left of my paw here," it indicated the instruction by lifting said left paw. "However, I must insist that your vassals travel behind me. It would not be dignified of an elf with my accomplishments to take up the rear. Not to mention that I have no intention of you trying something once you're clear with me still inside."

This was a bit of an inconvenience, but not one crippling to her plans. "Distrust is apparently not one-sided. But that is fair."

The chimera said nothing further on that score, and went back to instruction, "Unless the mountain has changed drastically over the years, which I doubt, a good path would be upwards and northwards at a ten degree incline. You... understand what I'm referring to, yes?"

Pirogoeth fought to roll her eyes as she picked up the scroll and slid it into her satchel. "Yes... simple mathematics *aren't* lost on me."

"Excellent, then let us begin. Do take the Heart, my dear."

Pirogoeth had used focusing crystals before, but certainly nothing of this size, so while she was used to the sensations she received, the intensity of those sensations were far beyond what she was prepared for.

From the moment she took the item in both hands, she was flooded with incredibly sharp senses unlike anything she had ever experienced. She saw the world more by its component parts, the infinitesimal faults in the stone walls around her seemed to glow, colors saturated to depths that didn't seem possible. The sounds of footsteps became orchestras of sound that she see could determine every distinct tone from.

The irony that she was having a hard time maintaining concentration while holding a *focusing* crystal was not lost on her.

It was by no means a pleasant experience, and one that reinforced her decision to proceed with her plan. Maybe the crystal would have been an immensely powerful tool to use against the Winter Walkers, but she wasn't sure she'd have the strength of mind to use it properly in a combat scenario.

The mage had to step over some residual clutter from the day's events to get in the position she wanted, then called back, "I'd suggest getting as much distance as you can at first. There's no telling what loose pieces of rock might break loose as I begin to push through."

Now, came the moment of reckoning... finding out if her spell would actually work as intended.

There were still so many things that could go wrong, even

though everything had come together to form *a* spell. A slight flaw in any of the runes that were inscribed onto the page could have potentially disastrous effects once she started channeling. Perhaps the drilling point wouldn't be sharp enough... perhaps it would augur in the wrong direction... perhaps there would be flaws in the shell that would cause the whole drill to collapse... perhaps there were improperly connected magical planes that could explode...

That *had* happened once with one of Socrato's prior apprentices, or so he claimed. It was supposedly a minor miracle that he hadn't needed to find the other half of his apprentice's skull and clean up a horrible mess of brain matter.

But, at the same time, Socrato also liked to tell her, "tentativeness and uncertainty is ironically the source of many a mistake in spell casting." He had enough faith in her studies to let her go out into the world. She needed to have enough faith in herself that it wasn't misplaced.

"My lady?" Azegbom prompted.

"Sorry," Pirogoeth apologized, "Just... gathering myself. Here we go!"

Pirogoeth closed her eyes, and channeled the energy from the scroll in her satchel and through the focusing crystal. Surprisingly for a spell *she* created, it wasn't particularly cooperative, the energy grudgingly leaving the scroll and forming into a shimmering translucent white conical drill.

It was equally unwilling to turn, like her magic drill was plagued by magic rust. Nonetheless, it *did* gradually get up to a proper speed that Pirogoeth felt was enough to test the mountain rock. The point bit in smoothly, almost like a knife into softened butter. It wasn't until the churning coils got into the solid stone that she felt much resistance, and even that was meager. Even ages hardened mountain bent before the manifestation of Pirogoeth's will, grinding to dust and being spit out to the sides as she bored to the drill's full depth and beyond.

"Hunh. It's working," Wiglaf grunted. "Wasn't expecting that."

Pirogoeth would have made a cutting rejoinder... if not for the fact that she honestly hadn't been expecting her spell to work as well as it was, either.

Directing the path of the drill was probably the hardest part of this entire plan, as the natural veins and formations of the mountain weren't always accommodating. It was a constant adjustment to keep the proper grade upward that allowed for relative ease of climbing. She could still feel the scroll in her hand, warm with energy, which was a tremendous boon, as it meant that the spell remained. If she needed to stop, she'd be able to cast it at least once more.

The drilling process was rather boring for *her*, and she could only imagine how tedious it would have to be for the rest of her party considering how slow the pace was. Hours of droning, grinding and slowly walking behind her and that gigantic chimera. They could have probably stopped for a spot of lunch, then caught back up within a handful of minutes.

Digging was taking so long, in fact, that no one thought it was the slightest bit out of the ordinary that she stopped, the drill disintegrating to nothing.

Aurora immediately ignored Azegbom's instruction to stay behind him and she rushed between his legs to the mage. "Pirogoeth! Are you okay?"

"Yeah," she replied tiredly, waving off concern even as Aurora helped her to her feet. "Just a little tired, probably a little hungry, and need to think about our next move. Jacques! Can you come up here for a minute?"

Azegbom was wary of the request, even as it didn't impede the former pirate from answering the call. "Why? What are you planning, arcanist?"

"How to get around this soft earth," Pirogoeth replied. "I think we might be getting perilously close to a magma chamber, and breaking into something like that could potentially end our quest right quick like."

That wasn't, in fact, a lie. She had indeed noticed that the ground beneath them had been slowly shifting to a more spongy, darker stone consistent with volcanic rock. She could also sense the chamber in question about thirty feet ahead. What wasn't the whole truth was that the chamber had been since dormant and posed no real threat other than a potential fall if she dug too close.

She even already had a plan to deal with it, but needed Jacques up there so she could give him instructions to disseminate without Azegbom becoming even more suspicious than he already was. "I trust we still have those climbing picks that you appropriated from Liga's stores?"

Jacques nodded. "Yeah. I was under the impression that the northlands might have some climbing to it."

"Well, there's going to be some climbing here too I'm afraid.

I'm going to have to take a sharper incline to get around this chamber. Make sure everyone has their picks secured because I might have to make some very quick changes of direction and I don't want anyone falling, got it? There could also be some falling rock if I have to change direction quickly, so if I call out to you, be ready to dig in and get as low to the ground as you can."

The sergeant nodded, though was admittedly . "Yeah. Got it. We'll be ready for when you move again."

She gave her team about fifteen minutes to get themselves situated, then yelled, "Okay, here we go!"

The second channeling of the spell was easier, but she could feel an electric heat crackling from her satchel as the drill was again made manifest. She was familiar enough with arcane material failure to know it for what it was, and that she most assuredly wasn't going to get another shot at this spell. While she supposed it would have been possible to double back and make another, the more time spent in Azegbom's presence was more time for the chimeric grand shaper's unstable mind to do something rash or unexpected.

She turned the drill at a much sharper thirty degree incline and more northeast than due north, gradually circling back towards the original destination and ascent once she was clear of the chamber. From there it was back to the tedium of drilling. At least the volcanic rock was easier to cut through, allowing her to pick up her pace and quicken the entire process.

Even then, it was still a matter of hours before she reached the point where her plan had to come into effect. Thanks to her expanded presence through the focusing crystal, she felt the terminus point before anyone could see it, and as the drill was prepared to break through the mountain and the open world, she encased the focusing crystal in a layer of ice and screamed, "Brace yourselves!"

Her team, to her immense relief had been ready and dropped into action, slamming their picks into the rock, wrist straps tightened, and pressing themselves as tight as possible to the tunnel floor as Pirogoeth's drill cleared the mountain, dismantling seconds later. The mage then spun around, anticipating Azegbom's charge, and hit it head on with a channeled hurricane gale that sent it tumbling back down the tunnel.

She eased up on the winds, then shouted to her no doubt disoriented team, "Go! Now! Hurry!"

Despite their shock, the team responded quickly, and that no one had been seriously harmed by Azegbom's forced retreat. Pirogoeth noted that Tyronica had taken what looked to be a nasty gash across the crown of her head to her temple, but that appeared to be the worst of it.

Azegbom charged, but Pirogoeth pushed it back again with another gale force. "You treasonous human!" the chimeric shaper roared as it slowly clawed its way forward, "Do you think to stop me with a hurricane? You can't cast forever, even with that crystal!"

"I don't need to!" Pirogoeth shouted back. "And you can have your damn crystal back! I don't need it anymore!"

Normally, the mage's throw would not have been particularly impressive. But caught in the vortex she had created, it carried right to Azegbom's feet, where Pirogoeth then sparked a finger of flame underneath the icy shell surrounding the crystal. The chimeric monstrosity paused for but a moment to glance at the artifact, just in time for the frostfire to ignite, amplified by the rupturing focusing crystal releasing its energy in one catastrophic explosion.

The blast alone would have been enough to kill. That it also served to collapse the tunnel merely would have ensured Azegbom's demise. Pirogoeth, however, didn't get much time to admire her work, as she was too close to the catastrophe to escape unscathed. She never even felt whatever it was that struck her in the middle of the forehead, the mage falling backwards and crumpling into a heap, sliding lifelessly down the exterior slope of the mountain before Jacques and Taylor caught her.

Chapter Six: Heart of Winter

So, what have you found?

The Dayne AI is scaling far too high, and spawning numbers far beyond what the event is supposed to handle.

Players are getting frustrated and are flooding the forums complaining about it. Fix it.

I've tried, sir. I've even tried to reset it twice. Someone is altering the code after the fact.

We've got a hacker?

Maybe, but we haven't seen any signs of infiltration. I'm sure there's a vulnerability in the servers, there always is after all, but unless we can find it and close it, this is going to keep happening.

Didn't someone mention something about a way of internally altering the code from the game client?

If you had admin access. But if someone is doing it that way, it's not through any approved admin command.

Didn't Hocico say something about admin access not deleting as it should?

On some occasions, but we still have ID records for those admin tools. If one of those legacy commands were being used, I'd know what account they were tied to and could reverse lookup from there to figure out where it's coming from.

Wasn't Hocico looking into those legacy admins anyway?

*She **was**, then she got locked out like everyone else. As far as I can tell, the only admin account that is still active is Bradley's, and he hasn't issued any commands in the last week.*

And where is Bradley?

Working from home for now. He's not even answering his phone. Last time we talked, he claimed that it was possible that whoever is hacking the game world could be monitoring all the admins and that he'd be going dark until he narrowed it down.

What the hell does Bradley think this is? International espionage? It's a damn MMO.

He's always taken this awfully seriously, sir. It's part of his charm.

What about Sam? Where's she been?

She quit last month. Remember?

Is her admin account still active?

Yes and no, sir. It hasn't been deleted yet, but it hasn't had any commands issued since she left. She's playing on a standard account now, but they don't even use the same e-mail authorization.

Any way to give her temporary admin access and see what she can do to dampen our aggressive event problem?

Presuming it didn't get corrupted right away like every other admin account, I'd still have to get authorization from Delvanno in order to give her admin tools on her standard account. You know how he is.

And he's on vacation until the end of the month.

Sir? Sam's party is actually completing the meta-event chain as we speak. It's possible that if they can complete it, despite the bugged AI, that this entire thing could resolve itself. Meanwhile, if Bradley finds anything and lets me know, I'll give you a call. I'm going to keep monitoring it from here and close up any holes I find.

Just... make it quick whatever you do. This might be our last big content update that gets us funding for an expansion. If it doesn't hit big, this game'll be designated into maintenance mode, and we'll either be reassigned or looking for new jobs.

Got it. I'll... do everything I can.

Better hope it's enough.

Pirogoeth had experienced enough subconscious scrying at this point to know that whatever she had just felt swim through her semi-conscious mind wasn't any mere waking dream. But at the same time, she had no earthly idea what half of the words that formed meant, what exactly was being discussed, or who those conversing were.

She groaned as just thinking caused her head to throb agonizingly, and that coupled with the movement of her hand onto her temple got the rest of the team's attention.

"Oh hey!" Goat chirped. "She's back! I wish I could have such a good night's sleep!"

Alyth no doubt punched him. "Somehow I doubt you'd consider what she went through to get to those hours of peace worth it."

"Thank the Coders!" Aurora said, hovering over Pirogoeth as the mage opened her eyes. "I hate it so much when you fall comatose. There's nothing I can do to rouse you, and I feel so powerless."

"I had been dream scrying again," Pirogoeth muttered weakly, reaching into her satchel and confirming that her black tome was in fact warm to the touch. "Not that I could make any sense of what I experienced." She blinked to try and clear hazy vision, and asked, "What happened, anyway? I remember collapsing the tunnel... then nothing."

"From what we were able to gather, a piece of the focusing crystal that you blew up hit you right between the eyes," Jacques informed. "Coders, we thought you were dead until Aurora assured us you weren't."

Pirogoeth brushed her fingers across the site of the wound, and felt the change from skin to smooth, polished, glassy stone. That would definitely explain the headache. "How..."

"It was lodged so deeply into your skull that we didn't dare remove it." Taylor explained, appearing into Pirogoeth's vision and kneeling down to her side. "Aurora thought it was a tremendously bad idea as well."

"I could feel your energy swirling about the shard," the healer added. "And remembered what you said about the dangers of breaking a mage away from scrying."

"If you're wondering, it turns out Wiglaf of all people has a delicate jewelcrafting touch," Tyronica said bemusedly. "After we had decided not to remove the shard, he grumbled about not letting you skewer your hand whenever you slapped yourself, and smoothed out the rough edges."

Wiglaf snorted. "It seemed prudent, and the rest of you were worthless on that score. Didn't even know the difference between grains of sandpaper."

Pirogoeth managed a weak smile, then raised an arm in silent query to help her up. Taylor complied, pulling her to a sitting position, and Pirogoeth gave a quick appraisal of the surroundings.

The first thing she was aware of was the fresh, cold and crisp air, of the smell of pine wood and sap. The colors of the borealis above in the brilliant night sky... ghostly strands of green and blue and white... so much sharper and more vivid than the pale wisps that she occasionally saw above Bakkra. The subtle differences in the temperature of the air, the barely perceptible changes in direction and intensity of the wind. All of these were things she had missed and could appreciate after at least a week buried in the stale, mostly lifeless underground.

"So... where exactly are we?" Pirogoeth asked.

"On the northwest face of the Forge of Creitus Mons, as the ancient people called it," Wiglaf answered. "The Mountain of the Forge of Creation. The ancient people had a like of many words to say little. Hrothstead, the permanent home for tribal gatherings and where the Winter Walkers hold dominion rest on the highlands to the southeast."

He looked up at the peak, largely cloaked by darkness. "There are three potential paths to our destination, none of them ideal. The easiest would be to trek south, and onto the narrow trade path from the western lands. But we will be exposed and our approach would be easily seen from undoubtedly the heaviest defended entry with whatever remained of their massive army."

Pirogoeth nodded, "Yes, I can see how that would not be ideal."

"The second would be to circle around the north side of the mountain, into the Upper Highlands, then follow the Unfreezing River south towards Hrothstead. While it is doubtful the river would be defended, the riverbank is treacherous going, the river itself is death of cold, and we would likely be exposed for some time to the absolute chill of the Icy Expanse. The river also flows northward into the Expanse, so we can't even use it for travel."

"And the third?"

Wiglaf exhaled sharply, and pointed upward, "The third would involve scaling the mountain itself, then down onto the grounds. It would offer near direct access to the Chambers of the Kings and is, on its face, the least treacherous path, though with its own perils. It takes careful climbing, and at the peak the air is stolen from your lungs. You cannot dwell long on those heights, or will you will suffocate. If we are delayed significantly in our path, it would no doubt be the death of us all."

95

Pirogoeth deferred to Jacques, and said, "What should we do?"

The sergeant looked at her with bemusement. "You really don't get it yet, huh?"

Pirogoeth blinked in response.

"It's your show at this point, girl. You've been leading this circus since we went underground, and you've got us this far. We'll follow *your* lead."

Pirogoeth became keenly aware of all the eyes upon her, yet the panic she expected to follow... didn't. Instead, she felt ready, like this was what she was supposed to be doing. With the confidence she couldn't understand why she had she declared, "Then we climb. We already have much of climbing gear ready as it is, and I think I have a few tricks to blunt the lack of air."

Jacques slid right into the second-in-command role. "Ya heard the lady. Break time's over."

He stood, the rest of the team soon following, and somehow Pirogoeth didn't feel the sense of smallness anymore. It felt like she was looking Wiglaf right in the eye as she ordered, "You know this mountain better than any of us. Take the lead."

Wiglaf nodded. "This face of the mountain is easier. It should not be a terribly difficult climb."

Pirogoeth remembered that during her studies. Unlike the Gibraltar Islands which were (or was in the case of the southern islands) very jagged and highly active volcanoes, the dormant volcanoes of the north had been less violent, their lava floes thicker and slower, leading to broader slopes with easier inclines.

"Easier" being the operative word, as Pirogoeth would not have ever described the climb as simple. It was still a significant ascent, with several cracks that were more than wide enough to swallow up a person and deep enough to insure they weren't going to climb out. The cold didn't help matters either, along with black ice that tended to accumulate where would normally hand and footholds.

She sincerely started to question the wisdom of this path especially once they entered the dead zone of the mountain. This phenomenon had been far more common in the taller mountains of the eastern continent of Xanadu, which had several such peaks, where the air thinned to the point that it became impossible to find the breath to sustain a person.

Mages had a handful of spells that were designed to counteract this, but Pirogoeth was increasingly worried that maintaining that spell for eight people *while* climbing would be more than she'd be able to handle. Without the safety lines that the team had tied between each other, Pirogoeth figured half of the team (including herself) would have died on the climb as it was. Could she handle the added strain on her mind to go along with the strain on her body?

A lot was stake that said she had to.

It was something she was so worried about from the moment she began the air compression spell that she didn't even realize that her hand had grasped the final ridge of the mountain until three other hands reached down to help her up. It astonished her because she didn't feel the slightest bit strained by the magical effort, even though her muscles certainly felt the climb.

Then after that, her thoughts were disrupted by the breathtaking view from their position at the top of the world.

The mountain top was in reality a frozen lake that had formed within the broad caldera of Creitus Mons, the ice remarkably clear and devoid of snow. This was both surprising and yet not, as Pirogoeth reminded herself that at these heights there wouldn't be all that much weather activity, and whatever there was would quickly get blown away by gale force winds.

Which led to the second discovery, a crystal clear sky unlike even what she had experienced several thousand feet below, this one illuminated by the rising sun in the east, casting a golden red glow onto the world below and the moon slowly fading under the increasing brightness. She swore she could see the Dead Lands from this vantage point, even though she knew that would be impossible considering the curvature of the world.

"Wow... look at that..." Tyronica whispered in awe.

Goat put his hands on Alyth's shoulders, the marksman surprising him by not reacting, and said, "Beautiful, ain't it?"

Jacques had been looking the other way, and pointed grimly. "That's not."

The party turned around, towards the north, and the Icy Expanse. While the glacial plain was pretty much what Pirogoeth expected, what gripped her with dread was the line as if drawn by a straightedge maybe a day's journey north, where the glacier abruptly ended, and where the violet haze and the eerily still dire water marked the edge of the Void.

The mage's heart fell. The Void was literally coming from all sides.

"Now, don't get *too* worked up," Jacques said. "For all we

know, it's been stable for centuries. The Gold Pirates have never been able to get a good look at the north side for any number of reasons. Let it be a reminder that there's a *lot* at stake here. So how about we stop using up our leader's magic juice and get down off this mountain?"

Pirogoeth was again reminded of just how little this spell she was channeling was taxing her. "Actually..."

She never got to finish her sentence when the world shook.

More accurately, the frozen lake shook then shattered, a coiled serpentine form, bloodied and roaring with rage as it lorded over the party that scrambled to find their footing on the shattered floes that teetered and drifted on the now exposed waters.

"What in the hells is *that*?" Pirogoeth grumbled as Goat helped her to her feet before she could slide off into the frigid waters.

Wiglaf shouted, "The Jormundgand! The last of the great ice wyrms! Legend said it slept in the bottom of the lake since the first freeze!"

Pirogoeth connected the dots. "And my little frostfire experiment woke it up, I'll bet!"

Pirogoeth wasn't sure what she was expecting the head to look like, but something resembling a frilled lizard was not it. At least, until the wyrm roared again, having identified its intruders, displayed several broken fangs as well as a majority of intact ones that were as large as she was.

That was more what she was expecting.

A pale blue glow shimmered up the length of its body underneath its blue-green scales, and Pirogoeth decided it wouldn't be a particularly good idea to wait to see just what it was. She countered with the largest fireball she could muster... which erupted from her hand with such force that the kickback threw her, Goat, and Alyth clear back onto more stable ground and into the caldera ridge.

The fireball crashed into the Jormundgand's icy breath, creating a second explosion that rocked the entire caldera, and nearly deposited the rest of the team into the water. It was only Jacques's quick action that kept Aurora from taking such a tumble, and Wiglaf had to make a similar save of Taylor as the corpsman spun perilous close to the ice edge.

"Coders, P, are you *trying* to get us all killed?" Jacques shouted as she pulled himself to his feet with an assist by Tyronica.

Pirogoeth didn't even try to muster an answer, instead stupefied by what had erupted from her hands. There was absolutely no reason that she could have conjured something that powerful so quickly, something that even staggered a great ice wyrm and caused it to topple unceremoniously back into the frigid waters.

She ran her right head through her hair to brush wet strands out of her eyes, then unwittingly came across the answer as her fingers crossed over the smooth glossy surface of the focusing crystal lodged in her forehead.

Could *that* be the answer?

Normally a mage had to actively focus energy through a crystal in order for it to amplify the spell being channeled. Could this crystal be so close to her mind that the process was happening unwittingly? Was that even *possible*? Or was there some other factor at play that she wasn't aware of?

"Heads up! Or... down, I guess..." Goat said, pointing down into the water. "Our friend's coming back up!"

"Everyone off the broken ice! Quickly!" Pirogoeth shouted. "Let's try and engage this thing on solid ground!"

Wiglaf was the only one not to heed Pirogoeth's order, instead bracing himself while gripping his club with both hands, eagerly anticipating the Jormundgand's reappearance. The mage decided not to humor him in this case, telepathically grabbing him by the back of the neck and throwing him towards the still solid ice on the caldera's edge.

The wolf shaman scowled in rage at her... at least until the Jormundgand burst up underneath the floe Wiglaf had been standing on, crushing the icy slab in between its unnaturally wide jaws.

"You're welcome," Pirogoeth snarled.

The wyrm readied another surge across its flanks and spit a large cone of icy shards down at Pirogoeth, that had remained the focus of its ire after the fireball affair. While she had been able to easily deflect or melt away the attack, she had to admit that it would be bothersome having to keep everyone underneath her umbrella of sorts.

"Spread out along the perimeter!" she ordered. "I'll keep it's attention on me! Be ready to move in when I call for a counterattack!"

"Move in?" Tyronica wondered.

"Easier to do than explain. Just be ready!"

The team complied, but as far as the Jormundgand was concerned, Pirogoeth was the only one to exist. This was a good thing... for now. As another icy breath attack clashed against her fire magic, followed by another, the mage was working out the pattern to its attacks. It could only take that breath so many times, and it was leaving a slight opening each with each attack. She had to time it just right... but if this worked...

She was channeling a lightning bolt the instant the wyrm's latest breath was vaporized by her fiery shield, the electric arc streaking across her predetermined path straight into the Jormundgand's mouth as it reared back to gather its strength. A broken roar followed as the beast was stunned, swaying backwards then falling forwards until its fall was caught by ice... the result of Pirogoeth freezing the lake again with an intense blast of pure cold.

"Now!" She shouted. "Hit it with everything you got!"

Jacques, Wiglaf, and Tyronica charged in, hacking at the neck and face of the wyrm, slowly gaining purchase in its tough hide. Alyth found some success with pinpoint shots that wedged through its scales, while Goat and Taylor eventually decided it was more effective for them to charge into melee range as well. Even Aurora was pitching in with the smattering of destructive magic she possessed.

Pirogoeth didn't dare do anything big out of fear of collateral damage, but she also got her licks in, slicing off thick layers of scales with blades of air... simply to reveal more scales underneath.

Jacques made a similar discovery, grumbling, "Are you kidding me? What sick Creator thought to give this thing *armor* under its *armor*?"

Even without that discovery, perhaps it was silly to think that they would be able to slay the wyrm in just one exchange. Pirogoeth called the party back to the perimeter as it began to stir, and again pulled Wiglaf away with mental force when he again disobeyed the order.

The Jormundgand thrashed, freeing itself and again shattering the lake, sending massive chunks of ice around the caldera. While the party was mercifully out of the largest pieces, Taylor wound up taking one large enough piece to the side of the head that it required Aurora's attention. While the healer rushed to provide aid, the wyrm dove deep into the extinct volcano, out of sight of even Goat's keen eyes.

"There's no way that's it..." the scout grumbled, peering as intently as he could to find any hint of movement in the deep waters.

"Because it's not," Pirogoeth agreed. "Be ready for anything."

Aurora finished with the potential head and brain damage to Taylor as signs of what was coming next started to slither onto the ice of the caldera's perimeter. Four smaller versions of the Jormundgand, "smaller" being relative as they were still eight feet tall at the smallest, pulled themselves up and made an immediate beeline towards the first target they found. Pirogoeth was able to immolate the one nearest to her on the right easily enough, but before she could address another a

100

larger problem that only she could handle towered above the party again.

The mage yelled, "Deal with the little ones as quickly as you can! It shouldn't take me long to disable our little friend again!"

Pirogoeth's assessment would prove to be slightly off the mark. The Jormundgand, despite it obvious wounds, was attacking with much more haste, each breath attack launching almost the instant the previous one dispersed. It was all Pirogoeth could do just to keep her fire shield up, much less counter.

Nor were the rest of the party exactly having an easy time with the spawn. They weren't particularly more vulnerable than their parent, especially since the party had to split up to deal with them. Alyth and Goat were having a particularly hard time keeping their distance, their arrows having little effect on the monster chasing them.

Knowing that Wiglaf was going to ignore her, Pirogoeth went with the next closest option. "Tyronica! Goat! Switch up!"

There was a brief moment where both wyrm spawn chased Tyronica and Goat, at least until Wiglaf's club convinced one spawn that it was a bad idea to ignore him, and Tyronica's flying shoulder tackle actually succeeded in toppling the other. With Taylor and Jacques managing to keep the third busy, there was at least some measure of stability on the current battlefield.

If only Pirogoeth could get an opening to shock the Jormundgand again... perhaps there was a different angle she could take here...

"Aurora! Do you know any lightning magic?"

The healer bit her lower lip and replied, "A little? You know it's not much."

"I don't need much. I just need you to zap this thing in the mouth when it gives an opening."

"I... can try..."

Pirogoeth had to hope that was going to be enough. "Alright, watch for the glow underneath its scales. You're going to want to begin your spell before the surge reaches its mouth, because it will take time for you to gather the energy, and the opportunity is not going to be large. Understand?"

"Yes," Aurora answered, her resolve firming into something approaching confidence.

Not that the healer would get a chance to try, as circumstance would quickly change the rules again.

The established pattern fell by the wayside the moment Alyth finally found a weak point in the Jormundgand's hide. The eye specifically, as one shot pierced through what proved to be tender flesh, spraying purple-colored blood violently and caused the beast to scream.

The Jormundgand turned its head towards the sound, just as Tyronica's sword finally found enough purchase to chop the spawn's head half off its neck. And that stirred the wyrm's ire away from Pirogoeth, launching its breath attack at the Aramathean soldier. While Pirogoeth was able to quickly shield Tyronica from the sub-zero blast, she wasn't able to shield Alyth from being hit by the splash effect, a shard of ice striking the marksman in the knee.

Alyth howled as the sudden stiffness in the joint caused her to fall over, then shriek in terror as the wound began to spread an icy film across her leg. Pirogoeth had heard of such freezing curses, but hadn't known any wild animal to be able to use such a sophisticated magical ability.

To make matters worse, Pirogoeth had to expose Tyronica to one breath attack simply to draw the monster's attention back with a fireball that crashed against the side of its head. While the sudden impact jolted the blast off-target, it was still enough to catch Tyronica's shoulder and infect the soldier with that same freezing curse.

So much for Pirogoeth's plan. With a growl, the mage ordered, "Damn it... Aurora, heal them!"

"Sorry!" Aurora replied in apology, like it was somehow her fault.

At least Pirogoeth now was prepared for the Jormundgand's behavior and was prepared for it the next time one of the spawn was killed by Wiglaf and Goat. Rather than a fireball, which she had cast more out of instinct, she grabbed the beast's head telepathically the moment she heard the spawn's death wail, and twisted the Jormundgand's head so that its breath attack crashed against her waiting fire shield.

"No... you're fighting *me*, got it?" She snarled.

Alyth attempted to offer Pirogoeth the interruption the mage needed, thinking that the eye of the Jormundgand would be a vulnerable much like its spawn was. It was a tough shot, especially from the marksman's stance and position, needing to fire an arrow with enough force to clear the wyrm's cheek ridge, but without too *much* force so that gravity would be able to draw it down into the eye socket rather than crash harmlessly into the upper ridge of the monster's brow.

Aurora was focused on Tyronica first, and understandably so, as the Aramathean's freezing curse had hit closer to vital organs, but the pain from that spreading curse was making concentration difficult. She figured she wouldn't get a second shot at this, so she had to make it count.

She did make the shot count, at the very least. It was near perfect, with precisely the arc she needed... but unfortunately lacking the power it needed to do any damage, instead pinging harmlessly off the wyrm's eyelid without even so much as earning the beast's attention.

In frustration, Alyth grabbed the nearest thing within arm's reach, and threw it at the Jormundgand. To her astonishment, the object in question pierced several layers of the monster's scale, so much so that it visibly recoiled, though the wyrm's attention was quickly grabbed back by another telekinetic pull from Pirogoeth. The marksman eventually identified the object by others next to it... teeth from the wyrm spawn that she and Tyronica had killed.

Aurora had finished curing Tyronica's curse, and had finally turned her attention to Alyth, distressing over how the curse had spread to almost completely engulf the marksman's left leg. Alyth ignored her apologies, and instead grabbed another fang and lobbed it towards Tyronica.

"Throw it at the snake!" She shouted, pointing up. "As close to the eye as you can!"

Tyronica tested the broken fang, and observed, "This... is not a particularly well balanced object..."

"I don't care! Just do it! Wiglaf! Goat! Do the same thing! Grab a tooth and throw it!"

None of the three ever actually hit the Jormundgand in the eye. Neither did Jacques or Taylor when they joined in. But what *did* happen was that the wyrm got poked by enough of its spawn's teeth that finally broke it's barrage to roar in rage... and that was when Pirogoeth gained the opportunity to stun the wyrm yet again and freeze it in place for another beating.

The team didn't even need prompting, charging straight in without delay, no doubt feeling that if they didn't finish this fight now... they wouldn't be *able* to finish it. Every ounce of energy they had left went into burning, cutting, slashing or shooting the beast. They were buoyed by the evidence of blood rather than scales, and worked into a frenzy similar to the flesh scouring fish Pirogoeth had learned about in the rivers of Canno.

And for a moment, it didn't look like it would be enough. The Jormundgand finally stirred, knocking back Jacques, Wiglaf, and Tyronica as it convulsed then slowly reared to its full height. But as the party tried to rouse the energy to prepare for another round, the mighty wyrm instead fell backwards, not even cracking the ice Pirogoeth had formed as it slumped lifelessly with its head dangling over the southern lip of the ancient caldera.

Jacques finally allowed himself to show some signs of fatigue, wiping his brow and breathing heavily. "Well, so much for the element of surprise. I'd wager the whole damn Daynelands heard that fight."

Alyth reminded, "We can't stay up here. P's gotta be exhausted as it is, and probably shouldn't be asked to maintain the air we need any longer than possible."

Pirogoeth didn't want to protest, mostly because even with her focus crystal enhanced might she *was* beginning to feel drained, and the biggest fight of her life was in the very near future. "I'm sure we'll find an opportunity to catch our breath a little down the mountain. It'll also be a descent, so it shouldn't be *as* hard on us as the climb."

The team took a wide berth around the corpse of the Jormundgand, sticking to the east perimeter of the caldera while Wiglaf examined potential paths for their descent. There didn't seem to be terribly many options. Much like the northern face, the southern side was astonishingly smooth, barring a handful of cracks or sharp jagged outcroppings. Pirogoeth somehow doubted tumbling several thousand feet would be any more pleasant on the descent as it was the climb.

"Well, Wiglaf?" Pirogoeth asked. "Any ideas?"

"We throw you down, see what happens, then follow the safest path."

Pirogoeth's brows furrowed in thought. Normally, this would be insane to even contemplate, but she was able to stop their fall underground with a burst of air. With her focused power... perhaps she could...

Goat tapped her on the shoulder, "Uh... P?"

The mage shoved his hand away. "Not now. I'm thinking."

He persisted with another tap. "Seriously. P."

Pirogoeth spun about angrily and shouted, "Do you want to be a test subject for my theory?"

It was only at that moment that she learned the dead Jormundgand was only *mostly* dead.

The wyrm was certainly on the edge of death, heavily bloodied and with large chunks of scale and flesh missing, but still had enough energy to rear up its head and attempt another icy blast. In a combination of frustration, rage, and uncertainty that she could protect everyone from whatever the Jormundgand tried to attempt, the mage threw caution to the wind and decided to eliminate the threat once and for all.

"Get down and brace yourselves!" she ordered as she quickly went to her fire tome.

The fireball she launched easily overwhelmed whatever breath the mortally wounded wyrm could muster, and vaporized what flesh had been stripped of its scales, reducing the great beast into quite literally a shell of itself. Then it fell with enough force to break through the ice and sink back into the depths for what assuredly would be the final time.

"So... that's it, right?" Taylor said tiredly. "That's really and truly it, right?"

Alyth growled, "Well now that you said that, it won't be."

And it wasn't. While the Jormundgand didn't come up... something else did. A blast of searing heat, and a steam eruption that Pirogoeth feared was the prelude to what would be a *true* eruption of the supposedly extinct volcano that they happened to be standing right on the lip of.

A slow descent was no longer an option. They had to get off this rock, and *fast.*

The burst of steam cast some chunks of ice hundreds of feet into the air. One larger slab didn't go nearly as far, dropping down not even fifty feet from the party, face up.

Pirogoeth had her plan.

"Everyone, onto the ice!" She exclaimed, pointing at the slab in question. "Use your picks to get a hold!"

If the team thought she was insane, they assuredly thought she was *less* insane than remaining on what was very likely an erupting volcano. They rushed to climb aboard their salvation, Pirogoeth digging in and wasting now time after hearing the chinking sounds of steel digging into ice, aiding the slab with a mental push to send it down the mountain slope.

And not a moment too soon, as the ejected ice was starting to fall back to earth, one such piece crashing close to where the team had just been standing with enough force to form a cracked indentation on the volcanic rock.

"Must go faster..." Goat whimpered as he looked over his shoulder at the destruction, and promptly regretted it.

Not that speed would be an issue, as the ice slowly melted and provided an increasingly rapid path down the smooth south face of the mountain. But moving quickly from the caldera merely introduced a different set of just as lethal perils.

"Everyone, lean left!" She shouted, not so much because she thought the weight would actually help turn the ice slab at all, but more that they'd be braced for the sudden movement right she took to avoid a large vent that had been due ahead. Not that she was able to give such warning a fraction of a second later as she needed to take a push back to the left as a chuck of ice fell down in their projected path.

The slab teetered perilously on the edge of the vent for far longer than Pirogoeth would have liked, and the panicked leaning from Taylor and Tyronica on that left edge wasn't helping nearly as much as they might have thought. Pirogoeth kept the entire thing from toppling over through sheer force of will, then once the vent finally fell away she forced that same slab down to keep it from skipping, needing all the friction she could muster for a hard right to avoid yet another falling ice missile.

That hard turn's momentum caused their makeshift sled to continue spinning, to the point that they found themselves looking up the mountain even as they slid down it, treated to one of the closest views any of them would want to an erupting volcano.

Not that there was terribly much to see, at least nothing like the cataclysm of fire and brimstone that common knowledge generally attributed to such phenomenon. Churning lava was barely visible over the caldera's ridge, occasionally burping small rivers of molten rock to dribble slowly down the mountain slopes, sometimes cooling to a stop within a hundred feet.

"Well, that's rather anti-climactic," Taylor yelled.

"I think we've got all the excitement we need right now," Jacques replied.

Pirogoeth rather agreed with the former pirate, righting their perch and stopping its rotation. While the slope of the mountain was easing, they were rapidly running out of space to slow down before they flew right onto the clan grounds, through them, and right off the ridge into what was much more jagged and unpleasant highlands.

"Hang on tight, friends!" Pirogoeth said, "This isn't going to feel good!"

She turned their ice sled directly into the path of the largest building at the base of the volcano, which she figured was the Chambers of the Kings that Wiglaf claimed the Winter Walkers held court. She figured the element of surprise was gone, so the sooner her team could engage the undead lords before every Dayne still in the region overwhelmed them the better.

Assuming they were in any condition to attack *anything* after this upcoming landing.

The mage did everything she could to slow them safely, but the crash was still severe, shattering the icy slab they had been riding as it slammed against the thick pine of the Daynish hall. Somehow the wall held at the point of impact, which was a blessing in the sense that it kept the team from being subjected to splintered debris that could very easily be fatal.

Not that it felt much better to collide with an unyielding surface. Pirogoeth mercifully felt something reasonably soft as she came to a stop, suggesting that her impact had been blunted by another member of the team, though she doubted that whoever she crushed would feel the same way.

She then fell onto the loose snow that had accumulated at the bottom of the hall, the depth nearly burying her as she dropped face down into the chilly fluff. That was then followed by another person landing on her, likely the same one that *she* had smashed into earlier. If so, it was only fair, she supposed. Sometimes, karma paid back quickly.

Of course, that didn't mean she thrashed like a wild woman to get out from under the increasing pressure of the weight pressing down on her. Someone stepped on her left hand, and her scream served to be the impetuous that finally got her free as the weight on her back rolled to her right. Pirogoeth pushed herself to her hands and knees, then a pair of hands looped under her shoulders to help her the rest of the way to her feet.

The good news was that everyone survived the crash. The bad news was that was the good news. Pirogoeth discovered that Taylor had been the one that had fallen on her, and that his lack of haste to move was for a very good reason. He had broken his right leg, the bone visible through broken skin and blood. Pirogoeth was astonished that he wasn't screaming, and instead was trying to set the break with clenched teeth.

She dropped down onto her knees again to help him, temporarily nudging Aurora away with the order, "Let us set this first, then I'll call you in to heal him. No doubt there are others would could use your help in the meantime."

Pirogoeth wasn't wrong. Tyronica had dislocated a shoulder. Alyth had a concussion. Goat had a gash over his eye, likely from banging heads with Alyth. Jacques had a severe sprain in his left ankle and knee. Wiglaf had a laceration all the way from his right wrist to his elbow, but he insisted that could wait as he could stand guard while the rest were attended to.

Pirogoeth attended to the less wounded after setting Taylor's leg, patching up Goat and Jacques while Aurora lent her skills to Taylor. When all that was finally done, Wiglaf allowed himself to be healed, and when Goat made the observation that had been overlooked in all the recovery.

"So... where are all the Daynes?"

It took a moment for the rest of the team to process the fact that Goat wasn't merely referring to the lack of any attackers coming to investigate what had been a tremendous amount of noise. He was referring to the fact that there wasn't any Daynes in the city *at all*. The grounds outside the Chambers of the Kings were devoid of any sign of life, racks of leather swaying in the wind, rotting food on spits hovering over burned out fires, as if the people working them had been abruptly taken without warning.

"You mean to tell me we could have walked through the front gate without incident?" Tyronica grumbled, sticking her head a Daynish tent and finding it as empty as everything else.

It was fortunate that there wasn't a Daynish presence, more than anything. While the mountain climb, thanks to the higher atmosphere winds had made the ground rather clear, the snow had accumulated on the highlands beneath it, drifts almost as tall as Pirogoeth clumped in some places. Simply finding an easy path was difficult enough. Fighting would have been nigh impossible for anyone involved.

As the team spread out across the meeting grounds, examining trader booths and nearby buildings for any sign of life, Pirogoeth had taken interest towards the south and the ridge that looked out towards the highlands. As irrational as it was, she looked out to the horizon for any sign of the war far off, or at worst any sign of the devastation the Daynes left behind.

"I doubt you'll see anything," Jacques whispered softly to avoid startling her.

She shook her head, "I... was kinda expecting to see smoke and burning land, even though I knew that wasn't likely. Just astounded at how from here you don't even see anything that's amiss." The mage pointed downward towards the flatland just at the edge of what could be seen, and added, "For example, if you didn't know the Dead Lands were right there, you likely wouldn't even think anything was particularly unusual."

He nodded knowingly, "There were points where I was out on the seas, and thought about just how small we were. Out there, you'd never see much but the seas and the occasional island. It's kinda hard to wrap your mind around how we're so little, and yet can do so much damage."

"I'm getting *really* unnerved by this, friends," Alyth admitted. "Where is everyone? Have they moved their operations?"

Pirogoeth had to admit that was entirely possible, if not likely. There was no way that the Winter Walkers would leave themselves undefended, right? "I hope they haven't," Pirogoeth said nonetheless, "because we can't afford a hunt across the Daynelands."

Wiglaf took position directly in front of the entry to the Chamber of Kings. From this side, Pirogoeth could clearly determine it's importance, far taller and longer than any other construction on the ceremonial grounds of Hrothstead. They were greeted by white fur splattered with dried blood covering the entry and seventeen severed heads mounted on spikes over it, dried from the chill to a sickly gray and thin strands of bleached hair.

"My people would mount the heads of challengers as a warning of their strength," Wiglaf said flippantly. "The Winter Walkers have been busy."

"Why?" Pirogoeth asked, even as she dreaded the answer. "How many are usually up there any given time?"

"Usually no more than ten or eleven. Contrary to popular belief, we normally don't attack each other daily, especially if the man currently holding the chamber is perceived to be strong enough to have ten or eleven kills."

"Well, that's not terribly out of the ordinary, then."

Wiglaf grunted. "I don't recognize any of these from my last visit three months ago."

And there the other shoe dropped. "Oh."

"I take it as an indication that the Winter Walkers still don't have the entire Daynelands under their heel," Jacques offered with an unusual optimistic take. "Might be useful for when we find them."

"Which is the problem, isn't it?" Pirogoeth asked. "Let's investigate inside. Even if they aren't here, maybe there will be some clues as to where they've moved to."

Tyronica and Wiglaf pulled the fur curtains aside, and Jacques stepped in front of Pirogoeth with his cutlass drawn. Not that he would have been able to see anything considering the dense blackness within. Pirogoeth quickly corrected that with a ball of light, then after she was able to identify where extinguished torches were lined along the walls, lit them with a snap of her fingers.

The entry hall was both precisely what Pirogoeth expected, and many things that weren't. Along the east and west walls were trophies of grand beasts, the stuffed heads of gigantic rockbears, bubble buffalo, and great serpents mounted onto lightly stained pine slabs in celebration of successful hunts. What was a surprise was the golden trim along the mounts for the torches, and blood red carpeting on the floor. At the far end of the hall to the north were two Aramathean stone sculptures of Phalanx soldiers complete with spears and shields, wearing helmets... and very little else.

"Barbarians of taste, I see," Tyronica grumbled.

Goat couldn't help but joke, "Are the male soldiers of your land *normally* that... um... equipped?"

Tyronica and Pirogoeth both replied simultaneously, "No."

"And how would *you* know *that*, huh, P?" The scout queried, his eyebrows twitching upward suggestively.

He received an elbow to the kidney for the trouble, courtesy of Alyth, but Pirogoeth shook her head dismissively. "I've witnessed the Imperial Games. They frequently competed in the nude." The mage willfully left out the part that she only could bear to attend one day of the week long event, and spent the entire time blushing so furiously that Taima joked about her propensity to sunburn.

"Focus," Jacques reminded. "Could we?"

"Yes, we should," Pirogoeth agreed. Now was not the time for silliness. She pushed forward between the two sculptures to a pair of ornate gold trimmed leather flaps that separated the hall from the next room. Tyronica and Jacques grabbed the edges, and looked to Pirogoeth for permission. The mage took a deep breath, nodded, then the team rushed in with weapons at the ready.

They had entered a near perfectly square room, sixty feet in diameter, lit unlike the entry hall due to a crystal skylight in the center of the steepled roof that allowed the winter sun to peek through, casting rainbow hues across the walls and almost covering up the blood stains that also marked the rough pine floorboards. Pirogoeth noted the two narrow tiers about three feet in width started at the perimeter, then about a foot drop, another three feet and another drop before the larger central level.

"This is the combat hall," Wiglaf explained when Pirogoeth asked. "The outer steps are for witnesses and this central area was for the combatants, used to settle differences or for control of the stead. If the Winter Walkers were here, this would be the best place to fight them."

She pointed to the north, where another hall beckoned, while this one was clear and displayed what appeared to be a decline and the start of a wooden stairwell. "What's over there?"

"The lord's chambers," Wiglaf answered. "That's where the Winter Walkers would be."

"And where clues where they are now would most likely be found," Pirogoeth concluded. "Let's go."

Pirogoeth had resigned herself to a long hunt across the Daynelands, a hunt that would cost thousands upon thousands of lives. At least until she was one stride from the threshold to the path onward when she felt the world almost turn in on itself in display of tremendous power that she could hear the reverb in her ears as reality snapped back into place.

At which point, the mage got a *very* close look at a Winter Walker.

The first thing she noticed was that it most certainly was an undead creature. The exposed bone of its spinal column visible through the rotted, cold-cracked leather breastplate right in front of her was evidence of that. It came with a bitter chill that forced Pirogoeth back, sneezing once as her nose was taken aback by the rush of icy air that she had breathed in.

That distance allowed her to get a better look of the risen Daynish king. It certainly had the stature of his former life, well over seven feet tall and what flesh remained glistened with frost and had the thickness of a man who had been of immense musculature. A surprising full head of long brilliant white shoulder-length hair topped a head framed with a solid silver band crown encrusted with emeralds, sapphires and rubies, as well as a incredibly lush beard except the right cheek that had been ripped clean to expose the jawbone and several teeth.

And the Winter Walker wasn't alone. The same warp that had brought the first in front of Pirogoeth had brought two others of its kin, appearing on the east and west perimeter of the combat hall. They were much like the first, dressed in decayed leathers that must have been remarkable at one time, though the one at the west was bald, it's crown tarnished unadorned gold, and missing his nose. The Winter Walker standing at the east wall had patches of bare skin under scraggly gray hair, missing his entire lower law, and it's right leg stripped clean to the bone from mid-thigh to the ankle.

Alyth had been quickest, raising her bow to attack the Winter Walker to her left, only to stop halfway, her eyes narrowing to dots before outright dropping her weapon.

Pirogoeth, aghast, demanded, "What are you doing?" At least... until she noticed the rest of the team had followed suit, dropping into defenseless postures where it looked like a stiff breeze would knock them right over, mere puppets on loosely held strings.

It didn't take the mage long to figure it out. This was the Winter Walkers' power of Domination. But how? They hadn't made any orders, or even attempted to impose their will. They hadn't even *spoken*.

It seems the littlest female is resistant.

Pirogoeth's head whipped to her right, her instinct telling her the telepathic communication came from that direction, the Winter Walker on the east wall.

An inconvenience, the northern one said. *She has what we want.*

Not much of one, finished the third. *She is no threat.*

Pirogoeth snarled, "Maybe not, but we'll see, won't we?"

Her hand slid into her satchel with practiced precision, expecting a flurry of fire that would at least give the Winter Walkers pause. But instead, she felt nothing. There was no warmth in the tome, no energy flowing into her fingertips. A second attempt with a different book also generated nothing.

Stupefied, she whipped open her satchel and stared at its contents, thinking that perhaps she had somehow mixed up the order during their travel down the mountain. That was not the case, everything was in precisely the right place. "W... what have you *done*?" Pirogoeth sputtered, looking back up at the Winter Walker in front of her.

Your magic has failed you. Now cease your vain protests, and surrender the Administrator's Tome.

Pirogoeth knew exactly what they were talking about, even if she had never heard her black book called such a thing. "You'll have to take it!"

Why? When we can have your former allies take it for us?

She then felt a hand on her shoulder, and it was pure instinct that got her out of Wiglaf's grasp before the Daynish shaman could clamp down on her. She spun away, only to be tackled to the ground by Taylor, and a frantic struggle followed which ended with Pirogoeth kneeing the corpsman in the groin and wriggling away.

The mage didn't get time to recover, getting tackled again before she could even rise to one knee by Goat, who grabbed for her bag a moment too late, as she tucked her satchel close to her chest, trapping it between the floor and her body.

That protection didn't last terribly long, as Taylor was replaced by Tyronica, who effortlessly dead lifted the mage off the floor and into a bear hug. Jacques and Alyth then grabbed the base of her satchel, and tried to rip it away. They nearly succeeded before Pirogoeth through blind luck if anything else was able to clamp onto one of the straps and hold for dear life.

While that resulted in a temporary stalemate, Aurora found a way around the dilemma, reaching for the clasp that secured the satchel's flap. From there, she would be able to simply take one or any tome she wanted. Pirogoeth grit her teeth, then howled in frustration, "Stop this immediately!"

And yet, it was *that* simple, futile scream when all else was lost that did the trick. Pirogoeth could see the light return to Aurora's eyes, the healer's pupils widening in recognition as she turned to the source of the mage's cry.

Those eyes quickly darted back and forth to the rest of her team. "What... are we doing? This... is the Winter Walkers! It's their domination! We need to stop!"

Pirogoeth had felt Tyronica's grip loosening as it was, and Aurora's order completed the turn, the Aramathean solider dropping her prisoner entirely, Pirogoeth falling to her hands and knees as breath filled her lungs again. Wiglaf clenched his teeth and rotated clockwise, focused on his foes, "I even *knew*, and I was taken off guard."

"They're as powerful as we suspected, they've even blocked most of my magic," Pirogoeth said grimly, pushing herself up to her feet again. "But follow my orders, heed my voice and nothing else, and we'll get them yet."

The little one has control of her own, what a fascinating development.

It merely means we must get our hands bloody. It is of no consequence.

They wasted no time demonstrating that they had good reason to be unconcerned. Wiglaf charged north, sizing up the Winter Walker that had in that same time taken a step forward, gripping his club with both hands as he took a right to left rising swing. It was a blow that had every right to shatter the Winter Walker's jaw and skull.

Instead, it bounced off the undead king, like Wiglaf had struck a ball of rubber. It was such an unexpected reaction that the Dayne paused to examine his weapon for any damage. By the time he had recovered to try again, the Winter Walker slapped the weapon away with a left backhand, then grabbed Wiglaf around the neck with the right.

The killing blow was so quick that Pirogoeth barely saw it happen. The mage had been expecting some grand show of strength. Instead, it simply bent Wiglaf's head to the point where it touched the shoulder, the gruesome snapping of bones and tearing of tissue happening all within a split second.

Alyth cried out in anger, trying to rush far too late to assist, and took her eye off the bald Winter Walker in the process. It would be a fatal mistake. The monster moved so quickly that no one could have defended Alyth from the blow, a swing of a spiked mace that crashed into her left kidney, crushing vital organs and sending the marksman flying into the north wall.

Alyth spun a half turn just before impact, and time seemed to slow down long enough for Pirogoeth to see Alyth's dead lifeless eyes, pupils narrowed to dots as it processed the last images to her dying brain. The mage was no longer even able to cry out in despair if she had wanted to.

This isn't right.

Jacques stepped to the front imposing himself between Pirogoeth and the approaching Winter Walker from the north. "Tyronica, with me! Goat, Taylor, get Pirogoeth and Aurora out of here!"

The mage felt a hand on her shoulder, but she was in such a dumbfounded haze that she didn't know whose it was. She was spun around just in time to see the third Winter Walker impose itself at the exit, it's massive claymore seemingly materializing from its back to its hands.

The relative slowness of the weapon was the only thing that saved Pirogoeth and Aurora, as both men shoved them back at expense of themselves. The blade went clean through their abdomens like they weren't even there, cleaving Taylor and Goat in two and depositing the parts with a gruesome arc of blood splattering across Aurora's vest and Pirogoeth's face.

This isn't right!

The mage turned again, to see Tyronica thrown like a human flail into the west wall, the force of the impact no doubt killing her instantly. Jacques had already been killed, his body crumpled over itself with his bent at unnatural angles under his torso.

She had assumed the Winter Walkers were powerful... but she hadn't contemplated the possibility they were outright invincible.

Behind her, she heard a crunch and a sick gurgle. She didn't need to turn around to know what it was, but she did so anyway. Aurora had stepped in between what had no doubt been an attempt on the mage's life, the rime-covered hand of the Winter Walker punching through the healer's chest and out the other side.

Damn it, this isn't right!

Pirogoeth finally had grown annoyed with her Chosen spirit repeating itself. Of *course* it wasn't right. But what was it going to do about the situation other than complain while everyone around her was being slaughtered? If that was all it was going to do, then she'd be better off being left to die in silence.

At this point, the Winter Walkers were taunting her, their voices echoing in her head, promising to make her death quick if she simply surrendered her black tome. They could end it quick regardless. In one last final act of defiance, she clutched the book tightly to her chest and dropped to her knees.

To hell with it. I know how to fix this. Damn stupid bugged event. Damn stupid buggy raid. Let the Admins ban me for doing their job.

Fitting that at the end of a "fight" that defied all proper sense that her Chosen spirit was choosing to abandon all sense.

The Administrator they had saved in Vakalm had said that the tome she carried would choose to express its power when the time was right. That meeting had been maybe a couple of weeks at most, yet felt like a year ago. It only came to her mind now because said tome had apparently chosen that moment to finally show what it could do.

Chapter Seven: Once More with Feeling

The black tome literally forced itself out of her grasp, rising just above her head and crackling with an energy that made her hair stand on end. The Winter Walkers recoiled from the display, and Pirogoeth decided to believe their reaction was one of fear. It emboldened her, and she reached up for her tome as the cover flew open and the pages starting flapping as if fingered by a swiftly moving hand.

The first page fell free of the tome, drifting downward to Pirogoeth's eye level before it vanished in a flash of white fire. While she didn't *see* any difference in her surroundings, she could *feel* one. The overwhelming sense of power had vanished in the Winter Walkers. Whatever had made them invincible and beyond any agency to stop had been ripped away.

The undead kings seem to know this too. *Stop her before it is too late!* The presumed leader ordered, but any advance they could make was hampered by the lack of inhuman speed they once possessed, and certainly not before the second page came free and similarly burned to nothing.

She could feel another difference, this of energy again building and flowing through her, an electric charge that shot through her body and centered on the shard of the focusing crystal in her forehead. Her magic had been restored.

She thrust out her hands to her sides, and with a mental push completely stalled a potential counterattack before the tome had finished its task. And it's final trick certainly was much more amazing and apparent than either of the previous.

The third and final page fell from the book, but instead of a small flash of fire, it erupted into a burst that momentarily filled the entire room with a brilliant light. It was gone with the blink of an eye, but what it left behind was a cadre of very perplexed, very confused, and very *alive* members of her team.

The black tome then unceremoniously dropped onto her head before falling to the floor, as inanimate as any other book, and that roused her from her stupor long enough to pick it up and stash it in her satchel again. Her stubborn tome was capable of reversing death itself. None of her colleagues had ever even *hinted* these books were capable of denying the natural world to *that* degree.

There... the encounter is reset, and they should be behaving normally. Now let's see what happens.

The Chosen spirit's voice faded into the ether once more, and its presence in her mind with it. While it would have been nice for it to just straight up deal with the menace, she supposed she shouldn't be terribly choosy. "Friends!" she called out, getting their attention over their understandable confusion. "We don't have time to ponder miracles! The Winter Walkers are still here and still formidable, but they are beatable! Form on me and let's finish this!"

They did that much quickly enough, Aurora and Pirogoeth forming the center of a circular formation as they prepared for the three foes that had regained their wits and readied their weapons, having been placed back in their original positions at the north, west, and eastern walls by the same fiery burst that had

"I have no idea what you did, Pirogoeth, but thank you," Jacques said from over his shoulder.

"Don't thank me yet," she warned. "The only thing I've done so far is given you the opportunity to die twice today."

"What's our plan, boss?" Goat asked Pirogoeth.

"Wiglaf, you know these... things... better than any of us. Which one represents the biggest threat?"

The wolf shaman pointed to the north, "Hroth is no doubt the leader. He was the first of the Daynish kings, and for whom this ground is named for." Then with a gesture to the west, he said, "Though Nossir is no doubt the greatest of our kind. It is said that he brought light to the north simply because the dark feared him." Then with a motion to the east, he finished, "Though you ignore Sagur at your peril. He was considered invincible during life, as only time proved to be his fall despite facing more challenges than any king before or since."

"Alright," Pirogoeth thanked, then issued her orders. "Wiglaf, you cover Sagur. Tyronica, keep Hroth busy. The rest of us, we'll work on wearing Nossir down. After he falls, we'll turn our attention to Hroth, then Sagur. Aurora, do everything you can to keep us standing. I'll help as much as I can. Go! Now!"

There was a reason for her strategy. As much as she was certain Wiglaf would have wanted another go with the first king of the Daynes, she figured that Tyronica's more defensive fighting style would be a better counter to Hroth. That assessment looked sound from her appraisal. Hroth was finding difficultly getting past Tyronica to aid Nossir, and even if Sagur wasn't taking much damage from Wiglaf, the wolf shaman's ferocity was effectively pinning the Winter Walker down.

Which left the rest of the team to bring down the Nossir, and as Wiglaf had predicted, it was not easy. Had Gongador survived the Battle of Liga, Pirogoeth suspected that it would have been far less harrowing to control the field. Jacques was a game front line fighter, but Nossir's raw strength was far more than he could resist for terribly long, requiring the use of the team to be constantly on the move lest they wound up being pounded into the floorboards like nails.

It didn't help Pirogoeth's nerves or spell casting that Nossir almost exclusively tried to smash her head like a melon, to the extent of ignoring everyone else save whenever Jacques could impose himself in the way. She supposed it was an effective strategy, as in Nossir's desire to squish her, the undead king was leaving himself open to attack from all other directions.

What spells she could manage to cast really didn't do much more than distraction than damage, like the fire flash that erupted in front of the Winter Walker's face, momentarily staggering him and allowing Jacques to once again step in to trade blows for a short time. That intervention proved essential, as Tyronica's scream grabbed Pirogoeth's full attention.

The soldier's spear had found what would have been a near instantly fatal wound to a mortal man, the weapon's shaft several inches deep into Hroth's right chest. Hroth had used that strike to twist his body to his left and downward and dislocate Tyronica's shoulder, though the Aramathean woman's discipline forced her to maintain her grip on her spear, finally pulling it free.

Despite what must have been considerable pain, she readied herself for another exchange. Pirogoeth wasn't going to give her the chance. "Jacques! Take over on Hroth! Aurora, heal her! Finish up this monster quickly, then turn your attention onto Hroth!"

Tyronica did not concede readily, until Jacques proved her need for first aid by pushing her away by her injured shoulder. Her strained hiss belied the pain she was in. Surprisingly, it was Aurora who lagged in her response, the healer needing another sharp order from Pirogoeth before she startled out of the deep concentration she was in.

"I'm sorry... but there's something... odd... about these men..." she tried to say.

Pirogoeth didn't *mean* to sound cross, though it must have come out that way. "Worry about it later! We need Tyronica's shoulder mended as quickly as possible!"

That got the healer in motion, and allowed Pirogoeth to focus on Nossir once more, which was fortunate as the Winter Walker again decided that she would make a lovely smear of organic matter across the floor. This was going to be a very critical handful of minutes, as she no longer would have the luxury of Jacques running cover for her when she needed it. One mistake in her positioning, one second where she misjudged her distance, and there likely wouldn't be enough left of her head for Aurora to heal.

The mage nearly made that critical mistake right from the start. She caught one of the steps near the perimeter of the room on her heel, and stumbled, and while that actually meant that Nossir's horizontal swipe missed just enough that she could feel the movement of the air in its wake, the undead king had her sized up for a downward chop.

She did the exact opposite of what would seem to make sense at first glance. She lunged *towards* Nossir, getting inside his reach, then diving through his legs, rolling onto her back as the Winter Walker turned to face her again. It was a perfect setup for a Flashfire spell, the small burst of flame erupting inches from the monster's face. While it did little damage, it blinded Nossir long enough for Pirogoeth to get some distance, and for Alyth to finally score a crippling blow, firing an arrow that ripped through half of his left knee.

Unable to support his own weight, Norris dropped to one knee. He swiped ineffectually at Pirogoeth once more, before Goat drove a sword pommel into the back of his head. Taylor followed with a slash that chopped though the Winter Walker's left arm just above the elbow, and Pirogoeth finished the job with a fireball that vaporized Nossir's head.

The Winter Walker's headless body fell backward, bent over itself, completely still. The sight invigorated the team, clear evidence that their enemy *could*, in fact, be beaten.

Pirogoeth didn't give the team opportunity to celebrate, even if they had been inclined to do so. "Everyone, move onto Hroth! Give Jacques some support! Tyronica, jump to Sagur when you're ready and Wiglaf can switch over!"

Aurora had worked quickly, despite her obvious distraction, as Tyronica took over battling Sagur within seconds of Pirogoeth's order. The healer was so engrossed looking back and forth between Hroth and the corpse of Nossir that Pirogoeth had to pull her roughly out of the way of the back swing from Hroth's greatsword.

"Aurora! If you're not going to focus, you're going to do more harm than good!" The mage yelled.

The healer sounded uncertain, even from what she was seeing that no one else could. "There's... something wrong... though. The flow of energy..."

"Worry about it later when there aren't undead lords trying to kill you!"

Aurora didn't protest further, but at the same time the only thing she did was step back into the southwest corner and continue staring down the already felled Winter Walker. At least she wasn't *directly* in harm's way. Pirogoeth figured that was something.

With that matter at least temporarily settled, Pirogoeth could focus once more on causing as much damage to her enemies as possible. With Nossir out of the picture, and Wiglaf and Tyronica running interference, it gave the mage a much more controlled battlefield and allowed her to use more complex spells in her arsenal. Undead flesh made for surprisingly good kindling, she discovered, so much so that she would temporarily call off Tyronica to hit Sagur with increasingly destructive pyrokinetic displays.

She even began to think that she'd destroy Sagur before the rest of the team brought down Hroth, and she voiced that thought with a cocky declaration of, "Fifteen gold pieces if I get my kill before all of you!"

"I'm not takin' that bet," Jacques declined.

"I will!" Wiglaf boasted, "I won't be beaten by some twig mage!"

Pirogoeth knew about hubris, and why she really should have chastised the behavior rather than encourage it. Especially when there were so many things that could still go wrong. But with victory so close, she let herself get lost in the moment along with the rest of her team.

"Pirogoeth! Look out!"

Not that Aurora gave the mage time to react to her cry, instead throwing Pirogoeth to the floor with a flying tackle. For a split second, Pirogoeth thought Aurora had somehow been dominated again, until she saw the ferocious swipe of Nossir's flanged mace going through where her head would have been.

The two women rolled in opposite directions as Nossir's mace crashed into the floorboards, ripping a massive chunk out of the lowest step in the process. Jacques responded first to run interference as Pirogoeth regained her feet, taking several strides back as she tried to sort out the battlefield once again.

How... how was that *possible*? Nossir's body was certainly not where it was supposed to be, nor was it missing its head any longer. She didn't get much chance to think about it further as the undead king shrugged off Jacques and again began his slow, dogged pursuit of Pirogoeth, forcing Wiglaf to step in as Jacques picked himself up off the floor.

Even as Wiglaf did so, Pirogoeth could *feel* the enthusiasm bleeding out of the team. It had been tiring just to get to the point where victory had seemed inevitable. Now they were back at square one. Truth be told, Pirogoeth could understand it as well. How could they kill something that wasn't going to stay dead?

"It was what I was trying to explain earlier," Aurora said, moving into Pirogoeth's vision long enough to quickly mend a cut the mage had most likely received during Aurora's tackle. "Their energy... it's not *life* energy... but whatever it is that gives them life... *undeath* energy, I guess?"

"Less theorizing, more explaining please!" Pirogoeth barked. She wasn't sure how much longer Wiglaf would be able to keep blocking Nossir's progress.

"The energy animating them is *the same*. It's connecting them. As long as one of them is alive, its energy can be used to reanimate the others."

"Are you kidding...?" Pirogoeth said in disbelief, but cut herself off as Aurora shook her head. Pirogoeth sighed, her mind wracking itself to think of a solution, or more accurately a solution that didn't have a good chance of killing them all in the process.

But try as she might, she couldn't think of any distribution of the team that worked. Jacques was a capable and wily fighter, but he didn't have the defensive discipline of Tyronica or Wiglaf's sturdy tenacity to hold up for the amount of time needed for a split party to do enough damage to bring the three monsters down together. She began to bitterly grouse that if Gongador hadn't been such a damn virtuously self-sacrificing hero, but stopped herself before she could besmirch his memory more than she already had. Bitter slander didn't help in this situation anyway.

But would they even be able to give Pirogoeth the *time* she needed in the first place?

"Pirogoeth? Do you have any ideas?"

The mage grimaced. "Maybe? I just don't know if we can pull it off. There's... at least one spell I could use... but I don't know if I can control it, or if the rest of you can keep the Winter Walkers off me while I channel it. I mean... look at us. We're exhausted."

Aurora smiled knowingly. "Leave *that* to me."

"What are you planning?"

"Something that I'm only willing to do once."

"That's not an answer."

"Because if I told you, you'd never allow me to do it."

"Well now that you've said that..."

Aurora shushed her. "No more time. If you have a plan, you have to do it *now*."

Pirogoeth growled before accepting Aurora was probably more right than wrong. She then shouted, "Okay, here's the deal! All three of them have to be killed *at the same time!*"

She momentarily worried about giving away too much to the Winter Walkers, but decided it was more important for her team to know what was at stake. "I have a plan, but it's going to take all of my concentration to pull it off! Whatever you do, you *can't* let them through!"

The mage then addressed Aurora quietly, "Okay... do what you need to do."

Pirogoeth went for her satchel as Aurora stepped forward, taking position in the center of the room. The mage was already deep into a channeling trance as the healer took a deep breath, held out her arms, then promptly collapsed to the floor.

Pirogoeth could hear the following panic from her teammates as muffled sounds. As much as she was worried for Aurora, she had already began to channel her spell, and breaking off now would be a delay that none of them could afford. She was committed and had to see this through as much as she could.

Though whatever the healer had done before she fell certainly worked. Pirogoeth could feel energy fill her fatigued bones, feel alertness and mental sharpness returning, things that she desperately needed as the magic began to churn like in an invisible mechanism with moving parts at multiple levels not even she could fully comprehend.

~   ~   ~

She remembered the very first time she had found the spell in question, and had brought it to her master's attention, because the runes had looked different, not tracing the work of a previous mage, but composed by the hand of whoever had been inscribing that particular tome.

"I didn't think you'd get that far so quickly," Socrato had replied. "Truly, I underestimate my apprentice at every turn."

"What even *is* this?" She asked, "What is it doing in a book of fire spells? Did *you* write this in?"

"I did indeed."

"Why?"

The venerable master bit his lower lip quickly, then pursed them. "When I was studying the practice of alchemy, I discovered a... primordial type of fire. A fire that burns hotter than even the heart of the volcanoes of this world. It seems to be locked within the heaviest of metals. Blood lead and mithril silver I found is the most effective. Even to this day, I don't entirely understand how that can be."

"And you put *that* in *my* tome," she said with a glower.

"I am not an elementalist by nature. But you are. An invoker with the potential to be Morgana's peer at the very least, no matter how much she denies it. I believe you *could* control this fire, in time and with considerable training to build your strength. In truth, I hadn't expected to have this conversation with you until you were *much* further along in your studies. But you have been such an incredible pupil, and I such a distracted master that I apparently have been blind to your progress. Forgive me."

Pirogoeth shook her head, "So this 'primordial fire' you scribbled into my tome, you honestly think I can use it?"

Socrato sighed, "I don't know. But I know that hiding knowledge from you isn't the answer. Much as I have to trust you with knowledge of domination, it'll be up to you to decide if this is a power you can or should wield. I have faith in you. I just have one bit of advice."

"What is that?"

"Don't look at the light."

~   ~   ~

Pirogoeth wished she had remembered *that* little piece of advice before she had dove too deep into channeling. Hopefully she'd have time for that instruction just before she released the spell.

And it was certainly a complex one. Her forehead was burning as the focusing crystal shard quickly became the focal point for the energy from her tome. Painfully so, but there was far too much for her to do before she could begin to use it.

If Socrato's studies were true, the only thing that would keep her and everyone around her from a quick and potentially excruciating death would be her ability to direct the primordial fire in her chosen direction, something that she'd only be able to do with force of will. A magical barrier would help somewhat, but the bulk of what would keep the spell under control was an active "push" from her mental strength. That took time to muster. And even when she was as ready as she'd ever be, she still wasn't sure it would be enough.

She reached into her satchel pocket and wrapped her fingertips around the piece of mithril silver that she had found on Azegbom's alchemy table, recognizing it by its shape. She feared it wouldn't be enough, even if Socrato's spell suggested it would be; if anything it would be too large for her to control.

If she failed, it wasn't like her team would have the time to admonish her for it... so *that* much was a small comfort.

Pirogoeth could feel heat building in the shard, exactly as Socrato's research had said. Her mind drifted downward and inward, focusing on a level so small that she couldn't even perceive it. She could only *believe* it was there, a level in which the shimmering metal she was holding could be torn asunder at its metaphysical state of being.

It was a task that required so much concentration that the sound of a Daynish war horn sounded like it was miles away. But it must have been close enough in reality for Jacques to frantically order someone to keep Daynes from charging into the Hall of Kings. Wiglaf volunteered in a whisper, and someone else whose voice came so quietly that she couldn't even discern it.

But the Daynish reinforcements would be too late. Pirogoeth felt the shift as the energy from her tome flooded the mithril silver, the heat rising so swiftly that she almost released it involuntarily. She could only control the flame for seconds more.

Her eyes flashed open, not even giving herself time to appraise the battle line. She couldn't afford to. "Someone grab Aurora and get behind me! Fast!"

Pirogoeth then shoved the smoldering piece of mithril silver into her copy of *Rodgort's Invocations*, throwing the book in the direction of the confused Winter Walkers as the channeling of the spell completed. The undead kings were obviously disconcerted that the mage's team had partially retreated, and why they hadn't immediately reacted to Pirogoeth's throw, their eyes following the book as it dropped in between them, then as it started to glow an angry and brilliant white.

At that point, Pirogoeth remembered her master's advice.

"Get down and don't look at the explosion!" she shouted at her team, then finally focused on the psychic push that she would need as Socrato's Alchemist's Fire burst in something that didn't look or feel *anything* like the fire she knew.

Chapter Eight: By Fire Be Purged

Pirogoeth quickly learned why Socrato advised not looking at the eruption. Even with closed eyes, the light penetrated her eyelids and blinded her. Then the roaring gale of super-heated air followed, a rushing onslaught that she only barely managed to hold back and deflect northwards towards her foes. She felt herself sliding backwards, and had the fire lasted a second more, she would not have been able to contain it any longer.

But, mercifully, the pressure dropped as quickly as it came, the power burning itself away. Pirogoeth dropped to her knees, panting desperately for air, sweat dropping off her brows like rivers. In just that handful of seconds, every muscle in Pirogoeth's mind and body had been pushed past the breaking point. She hurt *everywhere*, screaming in pain as she felt two hands clap her happily on her shoulders.

A cacophony of voices followed, cheering her, a mess of sound that made her head throb as much as everywhere else. It took far too long for her teammates to understand something was wrong, at least in her estimation, and when that jubilation turned to concern, she slapped angrily at the hands all over her and shouted, "I can't see, damn you all!"

The mage momentarily forgot she had gone blind when she heard Aurora's voice call out weakly, "Bring her over here. Let me see what I can do."

Pirogoeth felt a pair of hands loop under her shoulders, then getting physically picked up into a cradling hold before being moved what couldn't have been far. She was then set down onto the floor again, and a hand, presumably Aurora's gently covered her eyes.

The mage felt the crackle of static energy, and she asked, "Aurora, are you alright? Should you be doing this?"

"I'm okay," the healer said reassuringly, even if her voice didn't support her claim. "Tired... to be sure, but I'll live." After a pause, she added, "I'd rather not do that ever again, though."

"What *did* you do, if I may ask?"

"A raw essence transfusion," Aurora answered. "You... sacrifice your own energy to infuse others. If you're willing to give enough, it can even bring a person back from the brink of death. It's not a permanent solution, if your patient needs further healing, then it still needs doing, but it can stabilize a person long enough for that added work to occur."

The healer choked back a moment of sadness. "I... had tried it four times on Gongador before you redirected me to other patients during the Battle of Liga."

Aurora's hand dropped away, and to Pirogoeth's surprise, she felt her sight returning. Initially blurred blobs of gray, then splotches of red, then browns, purples, blues. Orange, yellow, then green followed moments later, and finally the picture before her eyes sharpened into distinctive shapes that she could identify.

Alyth, and Goat, and Jacques were standing directly over her, the latter offering his hand to help her to a sitting position. Aurora was slouched to her side, leaning on her left elbow, looking not at all like she should have been healing anyone, much less Pirogoeth's blindness.

"And *you* probably shouldn't be doing *that* again," the healer offered with a tired smile, raising her right arm slowly to point to the north.

Pirogoeth followed the finger to the north wall of the combat hall. Or more accurately, what *remained* of the north wall. Socrato's Alchemist Fire had vaporized all but scant few scraps of the panels in the corner, as well as burned away much of the king's chambers *behind* it, exposing the stairway down to the open sky. The edges of the blast were still burning from what must have been tremendous heat.

The mage wasn't exactly sure *how* she had managed to shield them all from such a frightening spell, but for the blessings of the Coders, she did.

"And just what did *you* do, if I may ask?" Aurora asked with a teasing lilt.

"A very dangerous spell that I was insane to actually cast," Pirogoeth said, awestruck by her own strength as she noted a trio of elongated black shadow-like marks literally burned into the floorboards where the Winter Walkers had been standing. "My master discovered it during his studies when he was younger. He was equally insane teaching it to me."

Jacques knelt down, and patted Pirogoeth on the head. "Crazy or not, it worked. And nothing else would have, I bet."

The mage was too tired to resist him on the gesture, as childish as it made her feel. She did manage a cold glare that got the point across, as the former pirate drew his hand away, and then offered it to help her to her feet. Pirogoeth spun around once to do a quick headcount, then asked, "Where's Tyronica? And Wiglaf? And Taylor?"

"You might not have heard it, but reinforcements started to arrive," Jacques informed her. "Wiglaf and Taylor went out to the hall to stall them. Tyronica just went out there to check in on them. But it *has* been an awfully long time."

Pirogoeth offered to help Aurora to her feet, though she good Goat and Alyth's assistance instead, and then the party tiredly left what remained of the combat hall towards the entrance of the Hall of Kings. They found Tyronica just outside the entrance, head down as if in solemn prayer, and they quickly discovered why.

Aurora threw her hand over her mouth to muffle her astonished gasp. In the courtyard that had previously shown no signs of life, there were thousands of corpses, Daynish men and women lifelessly sprawled sometimes two deep. Gray ash sprinkling down from remnants of the volcanic turbulence above mixed with a light snowfall to cast the surroundings in a drab gray muddy pallor.

Nearer to the Hall of Kings, was where the team found the first indications of people who had suffered more violent ends. Pirogoeth counted up to seventeen before she stopped, her eyes identifying Wiglaf.

The wolf shaman had apparently crawled towards the entry, falling face down a mere ten feet from the flaps, a trail of blood tracing his path from what had been the center of the melee. Pirogoeth rushed forward, her fatigue forgotten, showing a strength she had no business possessing whether tired *or* rested as she rolled the Daynish man over.

Seeing how he had been mortally wounded made her wonder how he had survived long enough to even crawl afterwards. The gash along his neck and trailing down to his sternum should have disabled him from shock in a matter of seconds.

Tyronica hadn't looked up from her mourning stance, more feeling Pirogoeth's eyes on her than anything. "I was far too late to offer aid. I arrived as Wiglaf drew his last breath. He said, 'tell the mage her man fought like a Dayne'... and that was it."

Pirogoeth's eyes narrowed in fright. Her head spun around on a swivel, looking for Taylor somewhere on the perimeter, not seeing anything that resembled him through the mass of bodies in the center. It didn't make sense... where was he? He wouldn't have been so stupid as to wade into the mess like Wiglaf, did he?

It was Jacques who tapped her on the shoulder, and did indeed point towards the middle of the grounds, accompanied with a morose assessment. "With these numbers, it would have made sense. They wouldn't have been able to hold a choke point from a bull rush. Charge in, draw as much attention as possible, and buy as many seconds as you can."

"No... no... no..." Pirogoeth chanted repeatedly, now identifying the slender form of the team's corpsman, his lower bodied buried under an avalanche of dead Daynes, his chest cavity had collapsed, splinters of his rib bones punching through his skin and the damaged leather of his chest armor.

The mage cried out unintelligibly, reaching into her satchel and yanking out her black tome, screaming at it angrily, "What are you doing? Revive them! Damn it! Revive them! I know you can!"

But the black tome remained dormant, the red eye dull without even a sheen of magic power, almost like it was mocking her and her pitiful orders. Pirogoeth clenched her jaw, growled, then decided she was done playing nice with this damn book.

Pirogoeth knew logically that offering more blood to her scrying was dangerous. It had diminishing returns to begin with, the pain keeping her grounded being more important than any magical connection it provided. But the mage was beyond logic at this point, willing to take whatever meager gains it would offer in exchange for finally breaking her irritating tome's will.

The mage drew a long, deep gash across her palm, seeping blood onto the cover of the book, barely acknowledging Aurora's cry as Pirogoeth dove into the most reckless scry that she had ever attempted. She really didn't so much immerse herself in the Code of the World as much as she burrowed through it. She ignored the path of least resistance. She wasted no time trying to find a weak spot in the ley line barrier. Pain no longer mattered, getting lost in the Code no longer mattered, her own death no longer mattered. She'd accept all of it if it meant finally overcoming the black tome's impenetrable secrets.

At some point, she went beyond where her master could prepare her for, plumbing to depths that he hadn't even dared attempt. What she was seeing warped into something she couldn't hope to describe, a clear image on a clear field, twisting around and about her, though she wasn't certain how she knew that, as her senses as she knew it had betrayed her. There was nothing at the end of the road... Coders, "nothing" wasn't even a good description of it.

She recognized this place. She had been here before, though never consciously. The dream state that her scrying had sometimes led her to. And where she heard voices again, bypassing her ears and forming directly in her head. Words that her conscious mind would remember.

Faggot bitch! Rez me!

You heard Sam. It was a one-time only deal.

She knew that second voice. She had heard it before. It belonged to the Chosen spirit that had attached to her.

You know how the rules work, Krack. This is a hardcore game mode. I only let Piro handle that one exception because the fight was very clearly bugged. I was able to muddy the waters as to who was responsible for that one, but another incident could get all of us in trouble.
Fuck you! I worked as hard as hell to get this toon to where I want it, and now because that assclown sent me off to get killed, I'm bent over?
I got killed too. You don't see me throwing a tantrum over it.
Yeah, well you got what you wanted. You got that little girl pussy, didn't you?
That's out of line, Krackow.
Eat my taint, fucker!

Clearly the Chosen spirits didn't always get along, and could get quite violent. Domina Morgana had suspected as such in the few times she confided in Pirogoeth, but the younger mage hadn't given much concern to those musings. Perhaps she should have.

There. I kickbanned him. Let him cause drama elsewhere.
He's fourteen. Let's not judge him too harshly.
He's old enough to know better.
You should have let me handle it, Sam.
Nah. You've never liked him, Piro. You'd have escalated the situation.
*Don't you get started with me, Zenith. You know **damn** well I didn't want you playing doctor with my toon, and you did it anyway.*
We don't have control over those fine details, Piro. Come on. You think so?

There was a pause in the Chosen spirits conversation that matched Pirogoeth's own worry. There was something about her spirit's inflection that made that more than a simple question.

What are you implying, Piro?

130

I'm not implying anything. I'm telling you to get the hell out of my channel too. And that anyone who tries to mess with my toon like you and Krack did, they'll pay a price as well.

Piro...

We're done. Let's get our loot and call it a night.

Pirogoeth could feel... something... filter out of the dreamscape, though she sensed that her Chosen spirit and the one called "Sam" still lingered.

I thought I said to leave.

Not until I get some answers.

There's nothing to answer.

Oh yes there is. What were you talking about controlling the specific actions of our toons?

Why does it matter?

Because only a handful of people should have any idea about that. And you're not one of them. So out with it.

What? The emotional stats aren't really that much of secret.

Yes, but manipulating them should be. You tweaked the stats of Wiglaf and Taylor, didn't you? How?

I'm not your hacker, okay? I didn't edit any values on your servers. I just... gamed the system to my advantage.

*And had them charge to their deaths. Jesus... you've manipulated **all** our toons, haven't you?*

Probably indirectly. I meant it, Sam. Anyone hurts my toon, I'll hurt theirs. I don't see how that's unfair.

Pirogoeth could feel every drop of her non-existent blood turn to ice. Her Chosen spirit was nothing short of a monster, casually and heartlessly sending anyone close to her to their deaths for any perceived transgression.

Pirogoeth fled backwards, not even sure if she *could* escape the dreamspace she had barged into, but desperate to get away from the menace that apparently could control her and anyone around her. She didn't *want* to hear anymore, even if it had anything more to say.

Mercifully, there was a beacon, a glimmer through the ether and the lay line she had found herself in, like a lighthouse that she identified somehow as Aurora's. Following it led her back to herself, the beacon proving to be the healer's energies working tiredly on the mage's hand.

131

"Thank you," she said, startling the poor, beleaguered healer.

Aurora sighed in relief, and replied, "I wasn't sure how dangerous trying to heal you while you were scrying would be... but you were bleeding so badly and I wasn't sure if you'd..."

Pirogoeth patted her on the shoulder, and began to say it was alright before she froze. Her head whipped about frantically between Aurora, the rest of the team, and the bodies of Taylor and Wiglaf, while she came to a chilling conclusion.

She couldn't let *any* of them get any closer to her. As long as any of them were near her, they could get hurt, and her Chosen spirit had shown no remorse at all about potentially killing them. She had to leave.

If she could slip away at some point, then disappear into the forests, that could do it. The only one who she had told about her plans had been Wiglaf. They'd never know where she had gone. She could slip way, cut straight east towards Kuith, and no one would be at all the wiser.

"So that's it, huh?" Goat said. "This the end of the Daynish Campaign?"

Jacques then said, "Maybe... but didn't Wiglaf say there were *four* Winter Walkers?"

Then a low, raspy voice from inside the Hall of Kings startled them. "The fourth Winter Walker made the very foolish decision of leading an attack on Tortuga. The Domina Morgana quickly corrected him of his error before making certain that he wouldn't be making *any* errors in the future. The Daynish Campaign is in fact finished, and it is unlikely we'll ever see another. Only a few scattered pieces of the Daynish tribes remain, and it is unlikely their people will ever recover in our lifetimes."

The voice belonged to a true giant of a man, a chimera of some sort judging from the cat-like eyes he had, though what particular breed of feline wasn't clear due to the tightly fitting headwrap that covered from his forehead to chin.

The chimera wasn't dressed for the cold; bare arms sticking out of a gray shirt that had seen better days, and long denim trousers with holes in the knees, though the man didn't seem particularly bothered by that.

"And how would you know this?" Alyth questioned, understandably skeptical.

Jacques answered for the chimera. "Oh, he'd know," the former pirate said warily, his uncertainty seemingly for a different reason entirely.

"A friend of yours from the Gold Pirates?" Tyronica guessed.

Jacques, meanwhile, hadn't taken his eyes off the new arrival at all. "Something like that."

Goat's eyes lit up, "Then maybe he knows about the war to the South! Tell us, did the militia make it to Wassalm? Did anything survive the Daynish army?"

The chimera laughed softly. "I will catch you up to goings in the south in time." He looked over his shoulder, back inside the Hall of Kings and added, "For now, you have spoils of war to claim. You've earned them."

He stepped aside to let the team pass, instructing them where to go. "Down in the private chambers. You can't miss it," he said before holding out a hand to Jacques's chest to stop him. "Hold a minute, old friend. I think you and I need to talk first."

The former pirate eyed the chimera suspiciously, then nudged Pirogoeth ahead of him. "Yeah, I think we do."

Pirogoeth grit her teeth in frustration. So much for slipping out from the back of the line.

But at the same time, perhaps she could snoop in on whatever those old pirates didn't particularly want the rest of them to hear...

~   ~   ~

Jacques had not been expecting to see Admiral Ahmin ever again after they parted ways in Grand Aramathea, much less see him in the heart of Daynish territory after one of the most most frightening wars of the modern era. As such, his first question was quite to the point.

"What are you doing here, Admiral?"

"Not an Admiral, for one," the tigerman replied. "And I'm investigating."

"Whattya mean, not an Admiral anymore? Did you get promoted? Demoted?"

"Neither. Still me, still who I am... just doing something different now."

Jacques didn't seem to like that answer. "Who's in charge of the Goldbeard now? I'm guessing Sunay?"

Ahmin nodded. "Did you think I'd leave my ship in the hands of anyone else?"

"Good. Girl's got a good head on her shoulders. She'll run it well."

"Already is."

The old first mate turned his curiosity to the second half of Ahmin's original answer. "So, what were you investigating?"

Ahmin's breathing slowed, taking several long, slow breaths before answering. "You know we've never been able to get good eyes up north. To see if the Void is encroaching."

"Hmph, if that's all you came up here for, I'll save ya the time," Jacques said grimly, jerking his right thumb over his shoulder to the north. "It's already here. Maybe a day's journey into the Frozen Wastes. I and this group of misfits got a real good look from the top of the mountain."

For the investigation Ahmin was supposedly on, he didn't seem surprised by that announcement. Instead the tigerman craned his head up and around over his shoulder, and asked with bemusement, "And you were up there... why?"

"Because that happened to be where we came out of the Great Underground Empire."

The tigerman gave Jacques a sideways glare. "I thought you retired because you wanted *less* danger in your life."

Jacques shrugged, "Apparently I don't know what's good for me. Oh, and just for added horror to go with all of this, the Void is coming up from *below* us too. We stumbled upon some dire water bubbling up from the depths. Fun, huh?"

If Ahmin hadn't sounded particularly surprised at Jacques's first mention of the Void, the second certainly did. "Really? *That's* more than a little troubling." He again looked over his shoulder, this time inside the Hall of Kings, and continued, "That makes her even *more* important than I first estimated."

"You saw that little thing she did with the Administrator Tome, I take it?"

Ahmin nodded, "I arrived just as she invoked it's power, or I should say the Chosen spirit following her. Her master had never been able to delve so deeply. If I had to offer a guess, there's something about her Chosen spirit that can act outside the Coders' authority. While I should be concerned of this... she might just be the best chance for our world."

"So that's the sort of thing those books are capable of?" Jacques asked.

"Yes, and why I think it's important that I have eyes I can trust watching her."

Jacques didn't like the sound of that. "Am I being recruited again?"

Ahmin shook his head. "No. This is just a favor to me."

"What if I wanted to go home after all this?"

The tigerman almost spit out a single guffaw. "First of all, you don't. Second of all, you couldn't even if you wanted to." He didn't give Jacques chance to question further, as he spun about on his heels, and gestured to his former first mate with a beckoning finger. "Come on, now. Don't want your allies to take *all* the spoils."

~ ~ ~

Pirogoeth decided that was her cue to get back to the rest of the party, and she did so as quickly as she could without making enough noise to draw attention to herself.

It defied reason that the private chambers in the Hall of Kings was still intact. But apparently being underground meant it avoided the catastrophe of Socrato's Alchemist's Fire.

That's not what Goat noticed first, however.

"And no one finds it at all odd that there's a random gold chest right in the middle of the room?"

To be fair, it *was* peculiar.

As Goat had said, it was a very large box chest with a curved lid, seeming forged from solid gold, from its panels to its trim, even to the lock that clasped the top shut. It was an insanely elaborate, heavy, and no doubt cumbersome thing that Pirogoeth had a hard time believing the Daynes would even *want*, much less *keep* in the heart of their territory. Gold made for a relatively *terrible* container considering there were any number of materials that would be just as effective, cheaper, and most importantly lighter.

"If I didn't know any better, I'd think the Daynes stole this from Domina Morgana," the mage quipped.

"Maybe they did," Alyth guessed.

"Not likely. We didn't see a trail of carnage coming in from the direction of Tortuga."

Tyronica, was understandably suspicious, a suspicion that she no doubt shared with the rest of the team. "That's... got to be a trap... right?"

Those suspicions weren't exactly quelled when the lock popped open without prompting, and the lid flew open, landing several feet away and nearly hitting Alyth as the marksman had circled around looking for any signs of foul play.

"I... don't *sense* any malicious energies..." Aurora said uncertainly. "But that really only means that any trap isn't magical in nature..."

Then Jacques grumbled bemusedly behind them, "So much for them cleaning out the spoils."

"Do you think it would help if I said the gifts were from me?" the large chimera accompanying him wondered.

"I doubt it. You look rather shady."

Mockery, at the very least, stirred the team's courage and forced down their concerns. Tyronica took most umbrage, as she was the first one to lean forward, the upper half of her body disappearing into the chest, followed seconds later with an awed gasp. She withdrew with a red painted round shield three feet in diameter with gold trim and the relief of a golden lion inlaid in the center.

"It's a Reahtan design," the Aramathean warrior noted as she rotated with the shield to test it. "But its lightweight for quick movement and allows for good coverage."

"The contents of that chest are spoils from previous Daynish Campaigns, taken from all over the world." the chimera explained. "For your bravery and your success in this troubled time. Some of the contents may be extremely rare and valuable indeed, some thought lost to antiquity."

Goat had dove in next, and he whistled with amazement. "Oh, Alyth dear. I think you'll want this one."

The scout emerged with a curved flat bow, the wood shimmering with silver, and the broad face etched with what Pirogoeth identified as elven symbols.

The chimera man gestured at the item. "Like that silverwood bow, crafted from the time when the elves still lived on the surface, and the old trees still grew. The string is actually from crystal spider silk, so I'd recommend some sort of protective glove before trying to notch the thing."

Alyth was dumbstruck as Goat handed her the bow, and she nervously tested the string before bringing her hand to her mouth because she had sliced her thumb. "I had thought I'd built up a nice callous by now. Gonna need special arrows made too, it would seem."

Goat had dove back in, "And here's one for... well... I dunno."

He held up a tapered dagger, glimmering with the sheen notable of Reahtan Steel. "Anyone want it?"

The chimera offered a recipient. "Aurora. I think you want

136

that."

The healer blinked. "I do?"

"Oh yes. That belonged to your mother, I believe."

"It *did?*" She said, gingerly taking the blade from Goat, who dove right back in. The healer rotated the blade off the tip of her finger. "My mother used this?"

"Reluctantly, and only after I insisted."

"You knew my mother?" Her eyes widened.

"We had met during a prior Daynish Campaign. She wasn't terribly keen on fighting, even as the Daynes pounded on her door. I pretty much forced her to take that knife, just in case, after my little band had finished fighting off a raiding party." He shook his head, "Oh those were the days."

Even Jacques was trying to fit that into a timeline. "When did you fight in the Campaigns? I didn't know our people were even involved in the last one."

"Oh, I'm referring about a time two campaigns and nearly forty years ago, before I even joined the Gold Pirates. Brings back memories. I was part of a ragtag gang not entirely unlike you all. Me, Richard, Vandriel, Rola, Stephon, Strali... heh... we even had our own mage, just like you guys."

Having a mage in an adventuring party would have been an oddity, especially in combat. Then even as now, they were an asset that would not have been willingly risked on border defense. "Is that right?" Pirogoeth asked.

The chimera grinned, the curve of his lips visible through the mask. "Yep. Girl from the barely tamed borderlands, named Morgana."

Pirogoeth's eyes narrowed into dots. "Morgana... as in...?"

"The Domina of Tortuga," he confirmed. "She's not going to be the slightest bit amused to learn you're following in her footsteps. Hell, you did her one over. Our foray into the Underground Empire was entirely by accident, and we sure as the black hells didn't linger long."

His voice then turned querying as he asked, "Just how closely do you plan on following in your kin's footsteps, I wonder?"

Did this chimera man know of her plans? If so... how?

Goat interrupted further discussion by chirping happily, "Oh yeah, this one's for me!"

He held up what seemed like a perfectly average leather vest. Sensing the lack of amazement from his teammates, he said, "Come on!

You clearly don't know Wolfen Leather when you see it! This is great!"

"I think it's your turn, old friend," the chimera said, poking Jacques in the side, then nudging him forward.

The former pirate gave the chimera a stern glare, but with a resigned exhale of breath, stepped forward and leaned into the chest. He quickly grabbed something that shimmered brightly, but quickly tried to bundle it up and tuck it into his pack.

"Hey, no! We gotta see!" Goat protested, earning him another glare.

Jacques said dismissively, "It's just a vest."

"A mithril chain vest," Pirogoeth interjected, amused by the former pirate's deflection. "Daynish tribal leaders and kings would wear those underneath their furs, as I understand it. No doubt a major reason why they seemed so invincible."

The former pirate clearly did not like the attention on him. His hand was diving back into the chest as he said, "Hush. Take your present."

He pulled out a narrow bladed sword and sheath, and dropped it into Pirogoeth's hands. The mage was initially startled by the lack of weight, until she drew the blade to discover that the blade was crafted entirely with mithril and was a bit narrower than the scabbard would have suggested. It wasn't as thin as a rapier, but still thinner than the usual fare.

Its hilt, and pommel were made from white gold, and the handle itself was wrapped in what looked to be a gray tanned leather. The cross guard was also forged from white told, with two bands; the top curving downward and merging with the lower upward curving band to frame a polished ruby etched to resemble an eye.

Goat again whistled, impressed. "Now *that* couldn't have been cheap to make."

"That's an Avalonian spellblade," Jacques explained. "Only ten of those were ever made, because they were expensive as all hells. Gifted to the old kingdom's most experienced and powerful mages. No one had seen one in almost fifty years at least. Figured they had all been lost or destroyed."

"Morgana had searched for *decades* after our adventures for one," the chimera man said, still grinning. "Not because it was of any use specifically to a mage. As I understand, it didn't actually amplify a mage's power, or was any more useful than any other weapon as a focusing tool. It was for the status, mostly, and that it was a finely crafted sword regardless of who used it."

Pirogoeth still wasn't exactly an expert with a sword, but liked having it for no reason than it would be something that would get under Morgana's skin. She unbuckled her belt long enough to position the scabbard just behind her dagger, then undid it again and used the belt the scabbard came with higher up her waist because she discovered the scabbard would drag across the ground otherwise.

She ignored the laughter that came from that discovery, hoping that the topic would shift to something else so that she could slip away unnoticed.

Then it seemed like she would get her opportunity. Goat addressed the chimera, and asked, "Okay, now with all the prizes give out, back to where we were. Can you give us an update on the war to the south?"

The shrouded man nodded. "The Northern Militia did in fact make it to Wassalm. And with reinforcements from Aramathea's Third Army, they held off the first siege. The Daynes will not get the chance for a second."

The chimera's choice of wording was not lost on Jacques. "Siege."

A regretful nod followed. "Everything north, west, and east of Wassalm... was razed to the ground. There was little time to call the outlying communities to safety in the city. As it was, the Northern Militia barely made it within hours of the Daynes pounding on Wassalm's walls. It was every bit of heroism the people could muster just to fight off the first attack. Had you been a day later, not even Wassalm would likely be standing."

Pirogoeth had taken three steps upon hearing that news, and the chill it gave her. Despite herself, she rotated back around and asked, "Bakkra?"

The chimera looked at her, and his slitted pupils widened, his eyes narrowing with sympathy. "I'm afraid to say it got hit hard. The people of Bakkra never saw it coming until it was too late. They didn't even have time to run. Last reports were that they were slaughtered to the man, woman, and child. Like everywhere else north of Wassalm, the Daynes didn't let anything survive."

The mage dropped to her knees in defeat. They hadn't been in time for anyone in the Northern Free Provinces. Her mother... her father... the entire town of her birth... potentially thousands upon thousands... dead. They hadn't been in time.

"We took too long underground," the mage whimpered, her eyes narrowing to dots. "We wasted so much time getting lost and doubling back... taking baths... we should have... we should have..."

"There was little chance those small settlements were going to survive after Liga fell," Jacques tried to remind her. "The fault is on the leaders in the Free Provinces not getting their heads out of their asses sooner to the severity of the threat. Not us."

The shrouded man agreed. "The fact that you ended this campaign *at all* is an accomplishment worthy of legends."

Pirogoeth didn't want to hear pitiful attempts at reason. They didn't understand. They *couldn't* understand. The mage forcefully shoved away Aurora's attempt to console her, and sprinted out of the Hall of Kings, turning vaguely in an easterly direction as fast as her legs could carry her.

So much for subtlety.

The view in front of her turned blurry from tears, and it was a minor miracle she navigated the eastern road downward into the thick forest of the highlands. She figured once she was in the tree cover that slipping away without being pursued would be easier.

The mage wasn't sure exactly how far she had ran, but it seemed like far enough once her legs finally started screaming for her to stop. She slowed to a walk for several minutes, and then after looking back to confirm she wasn't being followed, she stepped off the frost covered narrow trail and into the woods themselves, dropping down tiredly under the cover of a large evergreen tree twenty feet off the road.

She had forgotten who she was trying to get away from.

Pirogoeth couldn't have been in her hiding place more than ten minutes at best when she heard the rustle of a body dropping down on the other side of the tree. Startled, she jumped to her feet, and circled around, her new sword drawn and at the ready... only to confront Goat who was looking up at her smugly.

"How... where did you...?" She stammered while trying to demand answers.

He replied, "Ya know... you're pretty light and all, but you still leave tracks, especially in the snow, and especially when you're running. Not very inconspicuous, really."

A cough turned Pirogoeth's attention back towards the road, where the rest of the team was peeking above and around the foliage. "You weren't heading south, so we kinda started wonderin' where you thought you were going," Jacques said. While he sounded and looked amused, the rest of the team was showing evident concern.

What could she tell them? That she was cursed? That anyone

140

around her was in danger of being hurt or even killed? That they had been subtly manipulated by her Chosen spirit to be devoted to her? Would they accept that?

Could they accept that?

What would that knowledge do to them?

She inhaled slowly, deciding on a course of action. It was time once again to lie with the truth.

"I'm not going back to the south," Pirogoeth admitted. "Jacques, remember just before we were recruited in Bakkra, when I told you I had business in the north?"

The former pirate nodded slowly, but didn't say anything.

"This is the business I was referring to. My former master has tasked me to travel to the peninsula of Kuith, on the coast of the Eastern Forever Sea. As there is no reason for me to return home, it seems like the better part of valor is to simply... go there from here."

"By yourself?" Tyronica asked.

"It's not going to be exciting," the mage answered. "It's going to be me doing research of the ley lines. If you're looking for further adventure, following me around isn't going to be where you'll find it."

Jacques playful grin returned. "That's a funny thing, because as we were tracking you down, Alyth here said, 'Coders, I hope this girl doesn't drag us into more trouble. I've had enough for a couple lives now.' Ain't that right, Alyth?"

The marksman laughed. "I did. Truth."

Goat stuck his oar in, "It's not like *we* have homes to go back to either. And frankly, settling down somewhere that we'd be 'heroes of the known world' honestly would get annoying pretty quick, in my opinion."

The former pirate concluded, "So, with all that said, perhaps a retirement in some out of the way place might just be what we're all looking for. Did you consider *that* before you ran off on your own?"

Pirogoeth's face fell, and she slumped in defeat. There wasn't going to be any turning them away. The only thing she could do was to make sure she kept them at arm's length. It was the only way she could possibly save them from themselves.

When Pirogoeth spoke again, it was with the appearance of steeled resolve. "So be it. Just don't blame me when you're longing for some excitement while living on some frigid, rocky hell."

Chapter Nine: Foundation

It didn't even take the trip *to* Kuith before Pirogoeth's team began to realize the truth to her words. It had been a three week trek through the Daynelands, due to piling snow and the lack of people to clear the trails and roads. And even as they got farther from the heart of the Winter Walker's power, the reach of the undead monsters' actions could be seen and felt.

The Daynes were indeed decimated. Pirogoeth encountered at most twenty survivors during the entire trek east; two of them scavenging on the side of the path and quickly ran at the sight of armed southerners, and eighteen belonging to a family settlement far off the beaten path a week from Kuith that hadn't even heard of the cataclysm. The first question from the head of the family had been if they had any news about their regular traders, as none of them had come by in over a month.

Pirogoeth felt almost as bad for the surviving Daynes as she did for the survivors in the south.

And she almost felt as bad for *herself* once the trail reached its end; because they had to go *off* that trail another two days east to reach their destination. A land no one ever went or had any reason to be. One of the first things that she was going to need to do was have a damned trade line actually run to her keep, and it was going to have to be a pretty wide and well serviced one at that.

Coders, was she glad Socrato was footing *that* bill.

The scenery only would get increasingly barren from there, as the closer they came to coast, the fewer plants and trees they saw.

It quickly became clear why as the land dipped downward into what would become a massive flood plain in no doubt a few weeks time. Pirogoeth had known of its existence from her studies, and debated several possible ways to handle that problem with Socrato, but now seeing the somewhat manageable size of it led her to the conclusion that a bridge would probably be the best and most affordable way to proceed.

That valley then rose sharply again as it approached the sea, jutting out into a finger of land above the Eastern Forever Sea. Pirogoeth walked all the way to the cliff's edge where it formed a high fjord with a good one hundred foot drop onto some very deep, and cold waters. There weren't exactly going to be any summer beach parties in Kuith.

It also meant that it was going to be a pain getting supplies to the keep. Smaller ships could probably navigate the flood plain in the spring, but beyond that, ships were going to have a terrible time. The cliff face on any side wasn't broad enough for a practical boardwalk like the one at Grand Aramathea. Perhaps some sort of flue system that would power a lift or elevator would work, as it seemed that the waters directly under the cliff face would be deep enough for any size of sea vessel.

"Well, this is just a splendid place to set down shop, ain't it?" Jacques commented, turning himself left and right to get a full panoramic view of the surrounding.

Pirogoeth glared at him. The icy veneer she had settled on was becoming easier to construct the more annoying her teammates got. "I warned you. It's not my fault you decided it wasn't worth heeding."

Deep down, she couldn't blame him or fault his assessment. This stretch of land was probably one of the most inhospitable, drab, and lifeless places on the entire continent. Ninety-nine percent of the rest of the world would see the whole of Kuith collapse into the Void and not think anything of value was lost. To her and a handful of others sensitive to the swirling power from the Code of the World, its importance would have been painfully evident.

"That's not what I meant," Jacques said, jarring Pirogoeth from her thoughts. "I was referring to this place specifically." He pointed west and slightly north, to a tree line of the nearest forest a good half day's walk away. "Right there we'd at least be in reasonable distance to whatever supplies we could gain from the woods."

"No," Pirogoeth declined gruffly. "It has to be here. This is where the power is most concentrated."

"Fine then, but for now, until you can get the goods we need to build, I still say that we'd be better off setting up camp inland. Even if you had all the connections in the world in Aramathea, it'd be at least two or three weeks before their fastest ships or land beasts could provide anything for us."

That wasn't *entirely* true. Socrato could send at least basic supplies like food through void portals once Pirogoeth set one up. But Jacques was correct with his overall appraisal. It would be a long time before a keep at this particular location would be viable on its own.

The mage huffed, but relented. "Very well, lead the rest of you to a more suitable site and begin whatever foraging you think you can manage. I must remain here for now and make preparations to inform my master that I have arrived. I will find you by the end of the day."

If anybody on the team had become irritated, annoyed, or otherwise put off by the standoffish persona Pirogoeth had fashioned over the last three weeks, none of them had shown it until that moment. Jacques's eyes narrowed, and his lips pursed, as if he was considering saying something then decided against it. "Very well, ma'am."

He walked away, whistling to the rest of the team to get their attention, his orders becoming more muffled with distance. Despite that reaction being *exactly* the one she had been looking for, it still hurt. She hated having to push them all away. But it was for the best.

She *did* have matters to attend to that required her to be where she was, though.

The proximity to such an immense source of arcane power gave her the means to do many things with her scrying, like dig deeper into the black tome's secrets, but of more immediate use was the ability to use the Code of the World to communicate over tremendous distances as if you were in the same room.

Presuming, of course, that there was someone on the other end to listen.

It wasn't surprising that Socrato wasn't exactly waiting anxiously for her to arrive at the arcane gathering point that he and the other mages of the triad used. Doing some quick math in her head led her to the conclusion that it would be just after midday in Kartage, and that even if he *had* been waiting with baited breath for word from his former pupil he was quite likely getting some lunch.

So the young mage flared a signal, and waited in deep meditation. The flare itself really wasn't much more than a ripple that her master would "feel," at least if he was anywhere near his keep. After a second flare didn't garner a response, she began to worry that he *wasn't* in Kartage for whatever reason. Concern really began to set in after a third, then a fourth and a fifth...

Pirogoeth rather lost count at how many times she signaled before she got a response. Even worse was that it wasn't the response she was expecting.

*Coders curse it, which one of you asinine old men is making this ungodly racket... Oh. It's **you**.*

Pirogoeth was not expecting Morgana of all people to be the one to answer the call. *Hello... Morgana.*

The Domina of Tortuga took that greeting with all the respect

144

that it had been given. None. Pirogoeth could sense the irritation building before the older woman bit back whatever words she had been about to use. Instead, Morgana settled with something a little more subtly cutting. *Evidently, you have **finally** made it to Kuith. Took you long enough.*

Pirogoeth couldn't keep the smugness out of her mental voice, nor did she even try. *I do apologize for being delayed by the entire Daynish Campaign. You're welcome for stopping that, by the way. I'm sure it must have been a concern.*

Morgana snorted distastefully. *The Daynes were of no threat to **me**. In fact, you should probably be thanking me for drawing attention from you.*

*Yes, I'm sure that **one** Winter Walker must have been such trouble. I did have to face **three**.*

Pirogoeth was reasonably certain that a mage couldn't kill someone through the ether and the Code of the World, because if it had been possible, Morgana would have probably done it right then. And yet, showing a distressing lack of self-preservation, Pirogoeth decided to rub some salt in the metaphorical wound. *I found a most fascinating artifact in the spoils the Daynes had taken.*

Is that so? The Domina of Tortuga snarled with naked contempt.

An Avalonian spellblade. I was told you'd know something about them.

Pirogoeth swore she could almost see the Code of the World turn red, even as Morgana managed to rein in any emotion from her voice. *Magnificent weapons. Impeccably crafted. If you care for it, it will care for you for a very long time.*

Mercifully, another arrived to defuse the tension between the two women. *Ah, Morgana, did you summon us...* Augustus began before he processed Pirogoeth's presence. *Ah! My young lady, I see that you have arrived at Kuith! Splendid! Your mentor spent far too many hours fretting for you in the middle of that gruesome war.*

Did he now?

Oh yes. Dreadfully, if I may say so. Even news that the Winter Walkers had fallen, and by your hand at that, did little to quell his fears. Apparently, even without the Daynes, the frozen north can be a perilous place.

Pirogoeth decided to change the subject. *Did you see any trouble, Dominus?*

Oh, no. Donne and Reaht as a whole is too far south and east to see terribly much Daynish aggression, though I have no doubt it would have eventually found its way to our borders had you not cut out that foul army's heart. You have my gratitude.

Then finally, her old master arrived within the meeting point, clearly rushed as even his mental voice sounded out of breath. *Goodness me, there are some people that simply will not take no for an answer. Terribly sorry for the delay, now which one of you... oh!*

Tiredness turned to relief. *Thank the Coders you are well, dear girl. How is Kuith?*

Pirogoeth didn't try to pretty up her assessment. *It's cold and barren. Not sure what else you could have been expecting.*

Sounds much like Tortuga, only add 'wet' to the description, Morgana groused.

And Kartage was built on a swamp. I swear I had to rebuild it three times before it settled onto proper bedrock, Socrato added. *I dare say the only one of us who had a good roll of the dice was Augustus here.*

The Reahtan mage laughed. *Oh, on the contrary, dear sir and ladies. This perpetually sunny tropical island has no end to the number of aggravations in its climate. Truth!*

Socrato then got to business. *Now, I'm sure you need supplies and building materials and trade. I have three ships ready to go and several merchant caravans just waiting for the word.*

Pirogoeth didn't think she could have heard a more blissful declaration. *Consider the word given. Any food or camping materials that you can send quickly could also be of help. As I said, it's desolate here.*

I will do so. And I have the word of our colleagues that they will offer as much as they can as well. If you cannot reach me with any requests, either Augustus and Morgana can be of aid.

Augustus wasted no time acknowledging Socrato's words. *Absolutely. Consider me at your disposal.*

Morgana on the other hand, waffled. *I fear my keep took considerable damage during this last campaign. It will no doubt be of considerable expense to repair it.*

Pirogoeth could let that slide without another jab. *But, Morgana, you just told me that the Daynes had been no threat to you!*

The older woman didn't even attempt to hide her spite. *Why you little brat...*

Ladies! You are both lovely! Socrato interjected with a hint of displeasure. *Settle yourselves.*

Morgana huffed, and declared, *I don't see what more I am needed for, so I think I'll take my leave.*

Pirogoeth actually didn't want that. *No! Domina, please, I actually... need to consult with you on something. Alone. Once we're done here.*

Augustus found that unbelievable. *Really? Morgana? And you? By yourselves?*

But Morgana had sensed something in Pirogoeth's voice that had caught her interest. *Very well. I shall linger.*

Pirogoeth then addressed the three together. *I think Dominus Socrato has the right of it. These books might just be the key we need to fight back the Void.*

And why do you say that? Morgana queried, though Pirogoeth sensed there was an unspoken question somewhere in the older woman's words.

*During the fight with the Winter Walkers, they had been nigh invincible. They had killed every one of my allies, and were about to the same to me when my tome rendered them vulnerable **and** brought my party back to life.*

Back to life? Augustus questioned. *Are you sure?*

I watched one of them literally get her heart punched out of her chest and two others get literally chopped in half. You don't get much more dead than that.

Socrato was sufficiently awestruck. *Fascinating... I had suspected... but could never pry so far into mine...*

I think that is what I will do here. It's possible that with the strength of this ley line confluence, that it could give me the strength to bend this tome to my will. In time, at least.

Then our course of action is settled, Socrato concluded. *And I think that is a wonderfully suitable course of research for you. I also think that it is now time to officially consider you one of our number, and a master in your own right.*

Pirogoeth cringed at the thought. *Don't you think this should wait until I have an actual keep to be ruling over?*

No, I don't think we need to waste time convening again for something of the sort. Don't you agree that it's as good of a time as any, my friends and colleagues?

Indeed, Augustus agreed.

Yes, I concur, Morgana said, her mental voice still carrying that same sense of underlying meaning that was starting to unnerve Pirogoeth. What had the young mage gotten herself into?

Then it is settled. We are pleased to welcome you into our circle of archmages, Domina Pirogoeth.

She yielded to the inevitable, and merely said graciously, *Thank you. I will strive to live up to this honor.*

Now Augustus, I believe the ladies wish to talk privately, and it would be horribly bad manners to overstay our presence. Ladies, be good.

Always, Morgana said testily.

Augustus also offered his partings. *Morgana, Pirogoeth, may we speak again soon.*

Then Pirogoeth was alone with her most vociferous critic. *Now that the boys are away, what counsel could I possibly offer you?* Morgana wondered in the tone that suggested she already knew the answer.

Pirogoeth was already second-guessing this decision, but was already committed. No backing out now. *You've done the most research on the Chosen, so you would be the most likely one to know. Just how much control can a Chosen spirit impose on the person they are joined to?*

Pirogoeth could sense Morgana's knowing grin. *I see... you've delved **that** far, have you? You are just one full of constant surprises.*

Just how far have I delved?

The humor and teasing abruptly vanished, leaving behind the most sincere words Pirogoeth suspected anyone had heard from the Domina of Tortuga in some time. *You've heard the Dark Voice. A voice that chilled your very soul.*

Pirogoeth barely managed to squeak, *You... you've heard it too?*

Oh yes. Many years ago. Possibly even the same one you heard. I've not told many people this first truth. The Chosen spirits are not always benevolent, it's possible such kind spirits aren't even a majority. Many spirits are malicious and malevolent, truly despicable creatures.

Mine... I think considers me and those around me toys. Something to play with. It... manipulated those close to me, and guided two of them to their deaths.

Yes. They can do that. Not many have that power, but the ones that do I've yet to see them use it for good. The elder Domina stopped, and a very long, awkward pause followed before she continued. *Mine tried to use me to kill my allies, take their power, and use that combined might to destroy the whole of the continent and the world.*

Yet... the world is still here.

Morgana replied, *Yes, and it leads to the sole comfort I can offer you. Your Chosen spirit may be powerful, and it can compel you to do a great many things if you are not vigilant against it. But it **can** be resisted. You **can** reject its influence. It is not easy, it will not be pleasant, and your Chosen spirit will not accept your refusal, but you can fight it, and you can win.*

Pirogoeth wasn't sure she wanted to go much further down this path, but she felt she had to. *And that is the second truth?*

Dear girl, I think it is best if you discover those further truths on your own. For even if I tell you, I'm not sure you'll want to accept them. No one I've ever shared them with has.

That bad, huh?

Pirogoeth sensed the elder woman taking her leave with a parting of, *Farewell, Domina. My luck be with you.*

Then slightly fainter and dwindling to a whisper, *May luck be with us all.*

The End

Other works by Thomas Knapp

The Broken Prophecy

The Sixth Prophet

The Tower of Kartage

Dire Water

Fire Fox

The Daynish Campaign

For more information, visit http://www.tkocreations.com

Other works by Fred Gallagher

MegaTokyo: Volumes 1-3

MegaTokyo Omnibus Vol. 1

MegaTokyo Omnibus Vol. 2

Available from Dark Horse Comics

MegaTokyo: Volumes 4-6

Available from DC Comics

For more information, visit http://www.megatokyo.com or
http://www.megagear.com